AF192121

SHARON
LUTY

THE
Striddings

novum pro

This book is also available as e-book.

www.novum-publishing.co.uk

© 2024 novum publishing

ISBN 978-3-99146-310-8
Editing: Philip Kelly
Cover photo:
Philip Fiddyment I Dreamstime.com
Cover design, layout & typesetting:
novum publishing

www.novum-publishing.co.uk

Print product with financial
climate contribution
ClimatePartner.com/16547-2311-1001

Contents

October 1908

The night was cold. Her breath spiralled around her in soft wispy clouds as she made her way briskly along the woodland path. The moon was full and bright, it hung like a huge, illuminated bauble in the sky, and gave off enough light for her to be able to see her way. She could hear the river; not far to go now.

A fox barked in the distance and an owl hooted in a tree above her. Were they warning her? Was she doing the right thing? A moment of doubt crept over her. Then his face came to mind. Her heart told her she was right, no matter what anyone else thought or said her heart would not lie to her. She must follow her heart.

A pheasant, startled by her passing by, rushed out of the undergrowth in front of her screeching, its wings flapping. She jumped back in fright, her heart beating even more rapidly.

"Stupid bird," she muttered under her breath. Frightened by the bird's sudden appearance she lost her footing and slipped catching her skirt on some nearby brambles. She tugged it free impatiently and heard the fabric rip before the bramble branch swung viciously back and whipped her across the back of the hand.

"Damn," she said, and instinctively touched the back of her hand where it was hot and stinging, feeling the wet oily smear of blood. She wiped it clean with the sleeve of her blouse. It didn't matter now. She wouldn't need the blouse again after tonight, or the skirt for that matter.

She reached her destination: the summer house. She hesitated; would he be here? She couldn't bear it if he had changed his mind. The thought made tears well up in her eyes and her throat constrict. No, of course he would be here, she told herself.

She tapped lightly on the door. She held her breath, please let him be here. "Please," she said silently to herself "Oh please."

A slight movement inside, and the door opened. He was here. she felt herself breathe a sigh of relief and the silly tears in her eyes blurred her vision as he took her in his arms and kissed her.

"You came." He whispered to her.

She nodded, too emotional to speak and he kissed her again holding her so close they could feel their hearts beating together.

"Did anyone see you?" he asked.

"No. The moon is very bright, but I didn't see anyone on the way: I was very careful."

He released her from his embrace, and nodded, "good." He went over to the corner of the summer house and handed her a bag. "Here, you will need to change quickly, we don't have much time."

She took the bag from him and pulled out the clothing. She wrinkled up her nose. "Is this the best you could come up with?"

"Sorry. Didn't want to draw attention to ourselves."

She sighed. "I suppose. I had thought that you might have at least found me something pretty to wear. Are these your sister's cast offs?"

He chuckled. "I'll buy you all the pretty dresses you want soon enough." And mischievously grinning added, "You always look beautiful to me no matter what you wear."

She giggled. "Well, I hope you aren't going to stand there and watch me undress!"

"As if," he laughed and turned around so she could have a little privacy.

She started to undress when there was a ripping sound. "What are you doing?" he asked.

"A bramble has grazed the back of my hand. It's quite deep and won't stop bleeding. I'm just using a bit of my old blouse to bind it. I don't want to get blood on my new clothes, even if they are ugly."

Suddenly, they stopped and stood still like a pair of statues. "Was that someone outside?" she whispered.

Chapter one

January 1980

It all started with a letter. Not a sinister or malicious letter, but a simple little letter.

Sometimes, when I find myself alone in the house and a mist has crept down from the moor, shrouding the garden and surrounding land in a cold still silence I think of that letter. And once more I go over the frightening sequence of events that it triggered. I think then perhaps it would have been better if I had simply ripped it up and thrown it away.

But I have a curious nature and I know that would not have done. So instead, I kept the letter and acted upon it. And it was for this reason that I found myself on a cold wet pavement one late winter's afternoon outside the offices of Freeman, Walker, and son.

The office was warm. The icy wind that had been slicing into the flesh of my face came to an abrupt halt as the heavy oak door swung closed behind me. Taking my gloves off I walked up to the reception desk with far more confidence than I felt.

"Yes, may I help you?" asked a smartly dressed middle aged woman from behind the desk.

"I'm Miss Cromford," I said. "Miss Emily Cromford: I have an appointment with Mr Walker at three."

She smiled and took hold of a pair spectacles that were attached to a silver chain that was resting on her large ample bosom. She perched them on the end of her nose and looked at what I supposed to be the appointment book and nodded silently.

"Yes." She looked up, the position of the glasses on the end of her nose making her look slightly cross eyed and gestured to a brown leather sofa by the window. "Please take a seat Miss Cromford. I will inform Mr Walker that you are here."

I thanked her and sat down taking in my surroundings: a traditional solicitor's office tastefully decorated in soothing shades of green. Pale walls and a deep rich carpet with a soft swirling pattern, were complemented with furniture and fittings in rich deep oak, burnished leather, and brass, all polished to within an inch of its life by an over enthusiastic cleaner.

The view of the world beyond the room was obscured by a window of frosted glass, and the backwards blue and gold letter of the company name which was painted on it. People past by at intervals, hurrying along in the cold outside, their shapes blurred, their voices and footsteps muffled. Sleet tapped lightly on the windowpane slowly meandering its way onto the window ledge where it lay in grey soggy pools.

I unbuttoned my coat, and stuffed my gloves into my bag and pulled out the letter that I received the previous week.

It had been a Monday, trade in the flower shop where I worked was always slow on Mondays and given that it was a wet and cold January day, just two weeks after Christmas, and everyone was feeling flat after the festivities, and strapped for cash it was doubly slow.

"Put the kettle on Emily," Rita had shouted to me from the front of the shop.

"OK. Just need to finish tying off this ribbon," I called back. "They're to be picked up just after lunch." I finished the bow snipping off the ends with a flourish and stood back to admire my work. A beautiful spray of flowers in various shades of pink, starry, exotic looking tiger lilies and frilly carnations offset with pearl shaped rose buds in a translucent white all intertwined with the delicate green foliage of asparagus ferns. I wrote out the card that was to go with them:

> *To the most beautiful ladies in my life.*
> *Love Ben*

His wife had given birth to a baby girl in the early hours of the morning. He had called in on his way home from the hospital just as we were opening the shop. Drunk with the euphoria of his daughter's birth he ordered the flowers and asked that they would be ready for the afternoon visiting times.

I put the kettle on and wandered through into the front of the shop. "Kettle on," I said as I passed Rita and started to select flowers for a thankyou basket: Delicate yellow and white freesias, golden ivy and maybe some irises.

"Do we have any iris in the cold room; those tiny yellow and blue ones?" I asked.

"Flowers, flowers, flowers it's all you ever think about." Rita laughed. "Come and sit down have a drink of tea, and yes there are some."

She was right of course: my head is always full of flowers. When I am not at work arranging them, I am at home reading about them, and I am quite incapable of going out without stopping to admire a wildflower or a garden somewhere. This led to my other passion: painting. Water colours to be exact, most of which I admit were of flowers. Although I did do the odd landscape, it was the flowers I liked best. I loved the intricate details of them and of course their beauty. Each individual bloom, even of the same species had its own individuality – a personality if you will, and I aimed to capture that in my paintings. I sold them in the shop, although I hadn't intended to sell them. Rita had seen a few of them and had asked if she could borrow them for the shop to display on the walls. She thought they would look lovely with our flower displays and give the shop a fabulous Parisian chic touch. When people had started to enquire about them Rita suggested that I sell them.

"Emily," she had said, "they are beautiful pictures. People come in here because they love flowers so it shouldn't come as a surprise that they would like to buy a unique hand painted picture of them as well."

That was typical of Rita. She had fussed over me like a mother hen ever since I had started there as a Saturday girl well over ten years ago and I now worked for her full time.

I did as I was told and sat down to share a pot of tea with her when I remembered the day's post that was still in my bag. The postman was either early that morning or I was later than usual because just as I was leaving the house it dropped through the letter box, so I just scooped it up and put it in my bag and took it with me.

I went to my bag and retrieved the day's mail. Nothing exciting; a piece of advertising and another piece of what looked like junk, a brown envelope that probably contained some kind of bill and a white envelope with a company address printed on the top left-hand corner in deep blueprint. This was definitely not junk but I didn't recognise the company name either. I tore it open and began to read.

"What's that?" Rita asked amid a dunk of a second ginger biscuit.

"A letter."

"Well, I can see that." she said rolling her eyes, "but why are you scowling at it?"

I had no idea I was scowling, but I was puzzled. "It's from a firm of solicitors based in North Yorkshire." I handed her the letter.

"Dear Miss Cromford" she read aloud. "Please could you arrange an appointment with my office at your earliest convenience with regard to the late Roberta Cromford." Rita looked at me, "Roberta Cromford?"

I was about to reply that I had no idea when the shop bell jangled, and Eileen walked in. "Who is Roberta Cromford?" she asked taking her coat off and feeling the tea pot. "Good, It's still hot. I hope there is some left."

"Everything ok with the deliveries?" Rita asked.

Eileen nodded. "Traffic was hell, bloody road works everywhere. Thought I would arrive at the crematorium after the event," she grinned.

Rita frowned – "you got there on time though?"

"Oh yes, don't worry the funeral party were just arriving as I left. Rotten day for a funeral – mind you is there ever a good one? The flowers looked beautiful and there looked like there was a good turnout for the service given the cars that were arriving. Hope whoever they were gets a good send off." She took a slurp of her tea and reached for a ginger biscuit. "So, who is this, Roberta Cromford?"

"I don't know," I said. "I really don't know."

"Well, she must be some relative of your dads, you have the same surname, why don't you ask him?"

Rita glanced at me, "Emily's father is dead Eileen," she said softly.

"Oh, I'm so sorry Emily ..." she put her cup down. "I didn't ..."

"It's ok, Eileen. Really it is. You weren't to know and besides, he died an awfully long time ago."

It really was quite all right. Eileen had in no way upset me, but as much as I liked Eileen and her crass ways there were some things that I preferred to keep to myself; and my father was one of them.

Rita knew. She was the only person who knew how I really felt about my father. I couldn't even discuss him with my mother because of all the barriers that she had put up surrounding him. I had opened up to Rita around my eighteenth birthday, partly because it had been my eighteenth, and I had found myself wishing that he was there to share it with me. I think it also had something to do with being surrounded by all the wedding flowers that were for beautiful brides that were to be given away by their proud fathers, and those same proud fathers making speeches praising their beautiful daughters. All I felt was a tremendous sense of loss; I was never going to be one of those brides. Even though I had a good relationship with my mother, and I loved her deeply the void that was in my life concerning my father was always there, lurking in the background and I sometimes felt so alone and lost that the feeling consumed me. Not knowing where I had truly come from and who I really was made it hard to know where I wanted to go with my life.

All I knew about my father was that he had died of cancer when I was three years old. Those were the bare facts. Other snippets of information I gleaned from my maternal grandparents. He was Irish, had been an architect and worked for my grandfather and that he had been much older than mum.

13

I knew that I looked very much like him because I had seen a few photographs of him. We both had the same dark curling hair, and our eyes were a remarkably similar shape. Whether they were the same colour or not I do not know because the photos were of extremely poor colour quality and mostly in black and white anyway. My nose is smaller and rounder than his was and very slightly upturned. But our chins and mouths have a striking similarity and I notice the resemblance when I see myself in a mirror caught unawares and laughing.

There the similarity ends because my father looked to be very tall and there was something very elegant and refined about the way he held himself. It was very natural, and I knew from the way that he looked into the camera that he was a confident and relaxed man.

Tall, elegant, and refined would be the last words that I would use to describe myself. Refined may be if you want to describe refined as being quiet and I do not lack confidence. But as for tall and elegant well let us just say that a kind description would have me as dainty, perhaps petite, but never elegant.

I do not actually remember him though or him being ill and dying.

More a sense of something incredibly special no longer being there.

My mother and I went to live with her parents after he passed away. I don't remember moving either, only that things had changed. silly little things stuck in my mind. My bedroom curtains were now blue instead of yellow. My toys were in a different cupboard and the bed was by a window when I had been sure it was against a wall.

Of course, as I grew older, I started to ask all the usual questions that a child with one parent will inevitably ask. I knew my questions upset my mother, as she would visibly stiffen, and her beautiful soft grey eyes would cloud over making them appear even softer and somehow, she always managed to evade an answer. Because I knew that my questions upset her, and I loved her and didn't want to make her sad I stopped asking them.

I stood up, brushed the biscuit crumbs from my lap and took the letter from Rita. "It's probably nothing," I said. "Most likely a mistake, you know mistaken identity" and stuffed the letter back into my bag.

The afternoon passed pleasantly enough, serving customers with flowers, and making up and taking orders. We also began to discuss what we would need to order in for Valentine's Day. Although this was still a few weeks away it was a terribly busy time for us, and we both liked to plan ahead. We drew up a list of essential items that we would require such as ribbons and paper and roughly estimated the quantity of flowers we would need, and of course the variety that we would like. I mentioned that I had seen some tiny cupids in one of the stock catalogues and that they would look lovely in some of the arrangements, giving them a Victorian look for a different spin on the usual bouquet. Rita liked this idea and scribbled that down too.

As I walked home later that evening, I began to create beautiful arrangements in my head, but that letter kept creeping in. I walked past the marina, the little boats bobbing up and down, while the rigging made little tinkling sounds on the masts and considered if orchids would be too extravagant or perhaps just too expensive. And maybe how a combination of red fuchsia and tiny sky-blue forget-me-nots would look stunning in a Victorian posy: could I use one of the cherubs? I thought this last idea would have to be painted as it was just too impractical to have these two flowers in a commercial arrangement and thought about some preliminary sketches that evening when that damned letter drifted into my thoughts again. A chill wind was blowing in from the sea and it had stopped raining, I thrust my hands deep into my coat pockets, sighed and stopped walking. My bus stop was in sight but after a moment's hesitation I Instead turned around and walked in the opposite direction – towards my mother's house.

It didn't take long and all the while I was planning what I was going to say. The pain from my father's death had healed after all these years, but it was still a subject that we never talked about. And I was apprehensive now that I was about to bring it up. I was unsure how she would react, never mind if she could shed some light on the letter.

She lives in a neat row of modern houses. Each has a small garden to the front with an open plan design, making all the homes look alike. She had painted her door a deep blue, the colour of delphiniums my favourite flower, instead of the standard black that all the other houses had. I had planted up some flower tubs to stand on either side of the front door. They had been planted the previous autumn to give some winter colour and even in the gloom of the January evening the cheerful smiley faces of the purple pansies and the flame like shapes of the red cyclamen lifted the whole scene with a welcoming greeting.

I rang the doorbell and waited for her to answer. I heard her footsteps reach the door and then "hello, who is it?"

"it's only me, Mum."

She pulled off the chain and opened the door, a pool of golden light spilling out over the doorstep.

"Emily darling, what a lovely surprise." And then with a worried look "Is everything all right?"

"Yes mum, everything is fine. I hope you don't mind me just calling in?"

"No, of course not. I haven't eaten yet would you like to stay for something?"

I hesitated, I didn't feel that hungry, which was unusual after a day at work as it was normally one of the first things I thought about when I got home. This letter had really thrown me off balance, "I'll just stay for a cup of tea, thanks."

I went in and I took my shoes and coat off, putting my coat on the banister and went through into the living room. Mum behind me took my coat off the banister and put it on the coat hooks by the door and then straightened up my shoes. I smiled to myself – somethings never change.

We chatted for a few moments about this and that and when she brought in the tea tray I at last took a deep breath and said all in a rush.

"Mum, have you ever heard of a Roberta Cromford? I mean did Dad ..." my voice trailed away.

She glanced at me and set the tea tray down slower than necessary and then sat down in the chair opposite me staring at the tea pot.

"Mum. Are You, ok? I mean I'm sorry ..."

"Yes," she breathed. "It's been such a long time that you have mentioned your father that it took me by surprise that's all. Is this the reason for you coming tonight?"

"I know, and I'm sorry, but I have received this letter." I fumbled about in my bag and pulled out the crumpled envelope and handed it to her. "Any idea?"

She studied the front of the envelope and slid the contents out. She frowned slightly while reading but judging by her reaction to it also did not know who Roberta Cromford was either.

"Yes, that is rather odd" she said slowly handing me back the letter. I honestly can't recall having heard the name, but the letter is from Yorkshire, and I do remember that your father mentioned something about his family coming from Yorkshire."

"I thought he came from Ireland," I butted in.

"Well, yes: he was born there, and his parents lived there. His father worked on the docks or in a shipyard, I'm not sure which. You must remember Emily that I was much younger than your father and both his parents had passed away by the time we got married. Your father seldom spoke about his parents, but I got the impression that he had a happy childhood and that he loved them both very much."

"So how did you meet each other?" it was a question that I had so long wanted to have answered and I could scarcely believe that the opportunity to have it answered now had arisen.

"Well." There was a momentary pause as she leaned forward to put her teacup down with a little clink. She sat back in her chair with a small sigh and smiled.

"He came over from Ireland shortly after his parents died, to work for my father. He was an incredibly talented architect. They became friends and when Christmas time came around, he

17

was invited around to our home for the day as my father didn't like to think of him being alone over the festivities."

"And you met and fell in love?" I interjected.

"Well, yes ... at least I did."

She hesitated, but I was determined that this moment would not slip by. I had waited for too long with my curiosity bottled up and now it was like champagne, the cork had been pried off and the pressure from within released, spurting the contents into the air in a myriad of questions. The letter had given me a confidence that I had not had previously, so I urged her on because just like champagne one sip was not going to be enough.

She smiled at me and then said, "He was forty-three and the most handsome man I had ever seen." As she continued to speak her lovely soft grey eyes became even softer and her smile softened inwardly as she recalled the past. "He had dark curly hair like you Emily, and his eyes were of the same almond shape only they were a lighter blue than yours. He had laughing eyes, even when he was being serious there was note of amusement in them. My parents were alarmed when they realised my feelings toward him. I really couldn't see their concerns at the time but looking back I realise that they were only trying to protect me from myself. You see there I was a girl of seventeen in love with a man in his forties! He was only a few years younger than my own father."

"But they did let you see him, and they were happy for you?"

She let out a little laugh "Oh yes. They thought that it was just an infatuation and that I would grow out of it, and if I went out on a date with him that I would lose interest and then start to look at boys my own age. Your father found the whole thing rather amusing, and I suspect he was a little flattered that a young girl could have a crush on him. I think also that it rather disturbed him too.

He agreed with my father to take me out a few times in the hope that I grew tired of him. My parents trusted him to be a gentleman, and he always was." She glanced at me, her face colouring up a little, "much to my frustration" she giggled.

But the more time I spent with him the more I grew to love him, and he began to feel the same way about me, which made him extremely uncomfortable: he felt he was betraying my father's trust. He asked my father's permission to marry me before he asked me. By that time, my parents could see how happy we were together and if they did continue to worry about the age difference, they never let it show. Her voice started to tremble slightly. "I never once regretted my decision to marry him, not once. I know we didn't really have much time together and even if I could have seen the future, I would still have married him."

I said in a voice far too bright as I wiped the silent tears from my face. "Did you ever go to Yorkshire?"

"No, we never went," she spoke softly. "Perhaps if he had not become ill, we might have." She shrugged and said, "Any way," brightening up "I would have hated it: the only bits of Yorkshire that haven't been industrialised are sheep-infested bogs owned by odd speaking farmers, and it always rains."

I smiled to myself at that last comment. Now was hardly the time to tell her that that was a view many people had of Wales so, I said instead, "This Cromford woman – there is a possibility that she is some relation of dad's then?"

"Yes; it is a possibility. Look it can't hurt to give them a ring can it. By the looks of the letter, you may have been left something in her will – it does say the late Mrs Cromford, doesn't it?"

"Yes, yes it does. You're right. I'll give then a ring tomorrow. And thanks."

"What for?"

"You know, talking about dad."

She was quiet for a moment and then said in a voice that was barely above a whisper, "yes it has been nice."

A few minutes of silence elapsed between us, neither of us knowing quite what to say but finding comfort in our shared thoughts. It was mum who spoke first. "Let me know how you get on with the solicitor."

"Miss Cromford?" a voice said, breaking into my thoughts. I looked up to see a gentleman standing in front of me, his hand extended in greeting. "Peter Walker" he smiled.

He was a giant of a man. Not just tall but broad as well. His hands were like two shovels and engulfed mine in his handshake.

"I trust you had a good journey?" he said in a deep voice of flat sounding vowels that I had grown accustomed to since my arrival in Yorkshire yesterday. I told him that I had and followed him through into his office.

He was much younger than I had imagined, maybe in his late forties. He was clean shaven, and his hair was thick and dark with threads of silver running through it. He had such a warm friendly manner that my nervousness began to evaporate. He pulled out a chair for me and then walked round a massive oak desk and pulled out an equally large black leather chair for himself.

I sat down and before he had had chance to speak, I said, "Mr Walker, I feel there has been a mistake of some kind. I know that we have spoken on the telephone, but …"

"Let me assure you Miss Cromford," he interrupted with a wide sweeping smile revealing large tombstone-like teeth, "there has been no mistake, you are without doubt the late Mrs Cromford's great niece."

He opened a large beige folder on his desk and pulled out a handful of documents.

"Do you know anything of your father's family?

"Not really." I told him the sketchy details that I knew, mostly what my mother had recently told me and briefly outlined my childhood.

When I had finished, he shuffled about with the documents that he held in his hands, examining them closely. A slight frown crossed his giant like features every now and then. Before I could stop myself, I blurted out, "I'm the wrong Emily Cromford, aren't I?"

He looked up startled and laughed out loud, a deep booming laugh.

"No: you are the correct Emily Cromford! Everything you have told me does correspond to what I have here." He waved the papers he was holding at me. "Your grandfather, Edward Cromford was the brother of Roberta Cromford, so that does make you her niece – great niece to be exact."

"You are certain – I mean there is no mistake?" I asked, not able to believe that I had found a connection to my father's family.

"Quite certain ... it's just that ..." he hesitated unsure of how to go on. He frowned and then said, "To be honest I was hoping that you could have told me a little more about your grandfather and father. You see this firm has managed the affairs of Mrs Cromford for over sixty years and it was not until a few months ago that we knew of an Edward Cromford. It came as a bit of a shock to discover that she had a brother, not only to us but to her family as well."

Family! I felt an electrifying jolt run through my entire body at the word, a feeling of all my senses firing up at once. Family: I had never even considered the possibility of a family.

"Family" I breathed; "you said family?"

Peter Walker looked at me steadily. "I think," he said slowly, "that we could do with some tea."

Chapter two

I took a sip of the hot tea that a timid looking young girl with pale blue watery eyes had brought in. As I set the cup back in the saucer, I noticed that my hand was trembling. I said in a remarkably calm voice that belied my state of mind. "You mentioned something about a family?"

He looked at me thoughtfully, "Yes: The Maxwells. Mrs Cromford's daughter is married to Raymond Maxwell, and they have a daughter – Miranda."

"And Mr Cromford?" I enquired.

"Ah, there wasn't a Mr Cromford as such. When Roberta married, she kept her maiden name, she didn't like the idea of the family name disappearing and thought double barrelled names too fussy and pretentious. Her husband, an easy going fellow, didn't mind, he often referred to himself as Mr Cromford. He passed away a few years ago. He reached forward across the table and selected a custard cream from the pile of biscuits that the young girl had brought in with the tea. "Biscuit?" he offered me the plate.

I shook my head. "No thank you."

"Mrs Maxwell has also asked if you would like to stay over at the house tomorrow evening after the will is read; have I mentioned that there is a provision for you in the will?"

I was far more interested in the Maxwells than some will and now the prospect of staying over in their home seemed to be quite exciting.

"No, you haven't mentioned that fact, but I assumed that was why you wanted to see me."

"Yes, of course," he smiled, his dark eyes twinkling.

"I don't want to put anyone out," I continued, "but I would really love to stay over at their house."

"Good, I'll make the arrangements then."

I was about to question him further about the Maxwells when he said, "It really is a pity that you know so little about your father and especially your grandfather. Mrs Maxwell will be quite disappointed."

I was perplexed as to why Mrs Maxwell would be disappointed and was about to say so when the truth came crashing down around me. In my surprise that I had discovered a family, I had not taken in the fact that they also knew nothing about me, just as I knew nothing about them. And that my father, and grandfather were as much of a mystery to them as they were to me. Now I began to wonder not only what they were like but what they would think of me. My excitement at the prospect of meeting them and staying over overturned my excitement into anxiousness. Could I change my mind and say I wanted to come back to the hotel after the will was read? No, this would make me look like a silly child and certainly not feed my damned curiosity.

In my mind I had viewed this trip to Yorkshire as some sort of a pilgrimage, that here I would discover who I was, where I came from, and solving all my childhood riddles so I could find myself. How foolish I had been. All hope of finding the answers to my questions now lay in shattered fragments around me. Once more that door had been slammed shut in my face.

I needed a past to feel complete, to have a real sense of who I was; my past had been taken away from me. I had not only lost a father, but a mother too. For when he died a part of her seemed to evaporate away from me. I don't blame her, and I understand now that the only way she coped with her grief was to close down. She wrapped herself in an insulating blanket that not only shut out the world but to some extent, me as well. My mother's parents took care of us, and they were always exceedingly kind and loving towards me. I loved them dearly. But it was always my mother that seemed to get most of their attention. Perhaps, because I was so young, they thought that his death would affect me less and I think that if they had talked more openly about him then it would. These feelings made me uncomfortable; like a whingeing spoiled child, ungrateful for everything that she had. For all the happiness that I had in my childhood, and it was a happy childhood, there was this sense of loneliness. I never blamed my mother – how could I, she was only really a child herself and always the needier.

No, I buried that loneliness and lived with its strange influence until it became a part of me, buried deep somewhere in my subconsciousness. I barely acknowledged its existence anymore, a feeling of not knowing, not quite belonging but I felt its sharp stab now. For one brief second when I thought that I was to be handed a key to my past, to an elusive secret door; the door to my past and one that I believed, for one fraction of a moment that the Maxwells held, I felt hope. However, the Maxwells had been denied that key as surely as I, and had that door been slammed in my face, trapping my fingers in its rusty old hinges, the pain that I would have felt would have been no greater than the pain I felt now. I tried to speak but my voice had drowned in a sea of intolerable loneliness. I wanted to weep, cover my eyes and cry like the small child that I used to be.

Mistaking my quietness for puzzlement Mr Walker continued.

"It began last August, just before the bank holiday weekend. As I said, we have been Mrs Cromford's solicitors for many years – well my father had. This time when Mrs Cromford contacted us, she specially asked to see me and that she didn't want to come to the office or for me to go to her home. We arranged to meet in a café in the town. It was all very cloak and dagger and to say I was surprised was an understatement.

She told me that she had a brother – or at least she once had a brother and believed that he may have had a family of his own and that there should be some sort of provision in her will to take this into account. She asked me to trace her brother and told me the details of the new will asking me to draw it up as soon as possible. I did as I was asked and the following week she came to the office and the new will was signed. I hadn't had very much luck with finding her brother at that point, but she was convinced that there would be children and adamant that the new will replace the old.

He got up and walked over to the window. It was starting to get dark outside. The sleet and snow had stopped, and the sky was starting to clear reflecting the soft orange glow of the streetlights. He stared out of the window. He wasn't really looking, but absently gazing out at the evening sky and said quietly, "It was the last time that I saw her."

He reached for the cords of the blinds and with a soft slithering sound they slid down and the sky was gone. Turning from the window he once more sat down, his eyes dark and bright like two pieces of coal. "She died of a heart attack later that week. She had suffered from angina for several years, I believe that the condition had worsened with the attacks becoming more frequent, although she had kept that fact well-hidden, even from her doctor I believe. We were all saddened by her death. She had been a friend of my family for many years, and I had known her since I was a child. I had always been fond of her."

"I'm sorry," I mumbled, still too caught up in my own disappointment to say anything more and what he had just told me only seemed to add more to my confusion.

The last will and testament of Roberta Elizabeth Cromford was to be read at her home the following afternoon. Mr Walker had arranged to meet me at the hotel where I was staying and take me to the house which was situated in a quiet hamlet in the Yorkshire dales. I struggled to sleep that night. I was anxious about meeting the Maxwells but also extremely excited.

After the initial disappointment that they would not be able to furnish me with any more details about my father or grandfather, I concluded that instead of wallowing in this ridiculous self-pity of mine I should look on the bright side. I was about to meet an aunt and an uncle, and a cousin. Or were they all cousins? It really didn't matter what their relationship was to me. They were my blood relatives and they connected me to my father in a way I never thought possible.

It was the small hours of the morning when I finally drifted off to sleep. When I awoke, it was already starting to get light, and I realised with a start that I had slept in. I hastily washed, dressed, and rushed down to the dining room hoping that I hadn't missed breakfast. As I munched on a bowl of cornflakes, I hoped that I hadn't dressed too informally.

Yesterday I had worn a navy trouser suit: it was the only suit I owned. I had bought it thinking that it would make me look more grown up and professional. All it had done was make me feel awkward and uncomfortable. As lovely as it looked on the hanger it lost its appeal when I wore it.

Today I had chosen a cream-coloured sweater that had pale pink flowers embroidered down the sleeves in a soft trailing pattern and a pair of wool trousers in pewter grey and a pair of flat black leather boots. My hair was loose and curling about my shoulders, I had just secured it with a hair clip to stop it falling across my face, and I wore minimum make up as was the norm, just a little lip gloss and mascara. I did however feel wonderfully comfortable and relaxed: More me.

I had just finished my coffee when Mr Walker came in.

"Good morning, Miss Cromford, I hope that I haven't arrived too early."

I shook my head. "No, I have just finished breakfast. I'll go and collect my things." I had packed my suitcase the evening before, so it only took me a minute or so to put a few items in the case and to give the room a quick check that I hadn't left anything behind. Mr Walker was at the reception desk when I returned downstairs. He settled the bill and then took my suitcase and together we walked down the hotel steps into the crisp morning sunshine.

There had been a light dusting of snow during the night, but now the sky was a clear pale blue, and the air was cold and frosty. The wet slush from yesterday had frozen over and become hard and crisp with a pleasant crunch under foot.

"Mind how you go," he called to me "it's a bit slippery in places."

"Beautiful day!" he exclaimed as he opened the car door for me.

"Yes, it is wonderful," I replied as I slid onto the cream leather upholstery of the car. And thought how indeed everything really was wonderful.

We chatted little on the journey. Within minutes we left the bustle and noise of the town. Shop fronts became houses and houses became countryside. Soon we started to climb, and the landscape dramatically changed. Open moorland stretched everywhere while solitary birds circled above. In the far distance, imposing hills loomed over the land casting shadows, and dominating the skyline, their tops covered in snow and glowing in the morning sunshine like majestic beacons.

The land rolled into soft contours, at its upper limits empty hypnotic moorland which swept down into fields and trees. Little hamlets nestled together, lines of rivers and streams marked with bare branched trees that clung to their banks like silent sentries.

Secluded stone dwellings were randomly scattered and showed up dark against the brilliant white of the snow, while stone walls crossed this beautiful landscape.

I recalled how my mother had described Yorkshire as being nothing more than a dirty industrial bog and thought how wrong she was. This was a beautiful wonderland.

We began to descend from the moor and into one of the valleys – although they were known as dales here. Past a couple of farms and finally into a village.

"Not far now," Mr Walker commented.

I began to eagerly scan the houses trying to guess which house we would be stopping at when we took a sharp turn right and crossed the narrowest stone bridge I had ever seen. I breathed in and shut my eyes, waiting for the inevitable sound of metal scraping on stone, but none came.

Mr Walker chuckled. "it's ok, you can look now."

I laughed at myself and then he said, "It is a bit of a squeeze, I know. It was originally built when only a horse and cart were the mode of transport, but it still does the job." We drove for another few minutes and then took a turning from the main road and came to a pair of gates across the road.

The sun was shining directly into my eyes, so I pulled down the sun visor just as the gates were slowly opening.

I stared at those imposing black gates and felt my smile freeze, and my heart lurch, for wrought out of the iron work of the gates were the words: "Cromford Estates." One word on each gate, and each word painted gold.

Chapter three

"Cromford Estates!" I gasped and then looked at Peter Walker who was looking amused, if not slightly shamed faced. "Cromford Estates!" I gasped once more.

"I am sorry," he laughed "perhaps I should have told you more yesterday. But I do have a strict code of practice and you knew so little I thought it for the best."

His dark eyes were dancing with amusement, and I just couldn't be angry with him.

So, for the third time I said in an incredulous voice. "Yes: but Cromford Estates!"

"Are you going to tell me next that my aunt is a duchess or something and that I am related to the Queen!"

He laughed again and said, "No Emily. May I call you Emily? Your aunt did not have a title and you are not related to the Queen."

As we had been talking, I had not realised that we had driven through the gates and were now on a long winding driveway that was steadily climbing uphill. There had been thick rhododendrons at the gates entrance, but these had dwindled away, and there were now open grassed areas on each side of the driveway with beautiful specimen trees dotted about. They were mostly conifers; stately Scots pine and cedar, but some were deciduous, and I guessed from their shapes that they were a mix of copper beech and horse chestnut. We approached the house from the right-hand side, and I could see that the house was built on a hill side and appeared to be nestled in a natural basin. It was also not as grand as the name on the gates had suggested which came as a relief; it was more like a large sized stone-built farmhouse. To the rear of the house, I could see treetops and then the hill-side continuing to rise quite sharply until it met the sky where it turned into moor land. It was scattered with outcrops of rock that seemed to follow natural ridges. A few trees clung to these, but unlike the trees that grew on the lower levels these trees were small, twisted and bent, sculptured into gnarled shapes by the will of the wind. At the very top I could see huge grey like boulders of rock piled on top of each other. They looked menacing perched on the edge but they had most likely been like that for thousands of years so I put away the notion that they could topple down at any moment.

We pulled into a cobbled courtyard to the rear of the house which had not been visible from the road.

The courtyard was almost completely enclosed by a series of stables and stone outbuildings and the rear wing of the house which extended out across the back of the courtyard making it well protected from the elements. Some of these buildings had their doors tightly shut while others were flung open revealing bales of hay, buckets, and brooms. A chestnut-coloured horse with a white star on its forehead had its head hung over one of the stable doors, clouds of steam rising from its pink nose and lips as it snorted at us in greeting. The only patch of sunshine lay across the entrance melting the frost and turning the cobblestones to black glistening jet, the rest of the yard was covered in a thick layer of white frost. I shivered as I got out of the car and pulled my coat tightly around me and followed Mr Walker through a stone archway that led to the front of the house and out into brilliant sunshine. The view that greeted us was so beautiful I gasped.

I was stood on a long stone patio that stretched out over the entire length of the front of the house. There were tubs of winter flowers overflowing with richly coloured pansies and beautiful evergreen shrubs. Stone steps led enticingly down onto the terraces below until the terraces petered out and effortlessly melded with the lawns, and beyond that the entire dale spread out like a toyland. I could see the houses of the village that we had just driven through, smoke rising from some of the chimneys, while the river sparkled like polished steel as it wound its way through trees with skeletal branches. There were randomly shaped fields and several roads; I could see small vehicles moving along them, although I was unable to hear them, and there were several large ponds that seemed to connect to one another. A few clouds had bubbled up punctuating the sky, dwarfing the landscape, and marking the vastness of the scene.

"It's an amazing view, isn't it?" Mr Walker said beside me.

I just nodded, so absorbed in the beauty to say anything.

We went to the front steps of the house and up to the door. The house had the twisted stems of a wisteria trailing over it and rose stems were climbing up on each side of the door. It would look stunning in the spring and summer. I noted that the house must face south. I turned once more to look at the view my breath swirling and twisting in the cold air, intrigued by the way the garden blended in with surrounding land – it was hard to tell where each began and ended. Only to the west was a clear boundary and this was marked by a long bank of thick conifers and poplars. These must have been planted years ago to protect the garden from strong winds. The house itself would protect the front gardens and there was a natural wood that grew toward the east so surrounding the garden and creating a microclimate.

I heard the doorbell ring and turned to face the double doors of the front entrance. They were made of light oak and in the top of each door was a window and around each window was a stained glass insert of red roses and trailing green leaves. I peered through the glass to see a wide hallway. There was an enormous coat rack that was festooned with a large array of coats, several umbrellas and an assortment of scarves, hats, and gloves. Underneath that there was a neat row of shoes, boots, and wellingtons.

A large open fire was glowing in a fireplace on the opposite side of the hall, and I could see the foot of a wide sweeping staircase that was central to the hallway. From out of the shadows of what appeared to be a passageway towards the back of the house a black speckled dog that looked to be a spaniel hurtled towards us. It was wagging its tail furiously and barking excitedly. Close on its heels was a black dog, it lolloped along also wagging its tail and barged into the spaniel toppling it off balance sending the smaller dog careering into the wall. Undeterred, it righted itself and raced on to reach the front door the same time as the other dog that I could now see was a labrador. I heard a woman's voice call out. She was talking to the dogs and trying to calm them down, the spaniel was now leaping up and down with excitement like a demented gazelle. The owner of the voice came into view, waved at us, and smiled. As she got closer, I could see that she was a small roundish woman with very dark hair that was cropped close to her head. There were traces of white through her hair, but her fringe was silver and was swept across her forehead. She stopped abruptly and in a commanding voice said to the dogs "BED!" And pointed with her finger down the hallway from where the dogs had come. They became quiet and slunk sulkily away in the general direction from where they had come. Satisfied that she them under control she waved at us once more and then came to open the door.

"Hello, come on in, you must be both frozen stood out there."

She fussed about taking our coats and talked about the weather and the trip, her accent was very broad, and I struggled to catch just what she said. One of the dogs had crept back from where it had been sent and was now sniffing at my feet and wagging its tail. I bent down to stroke it.

"Emily, I would like you to meet Janice Parkin. The treasure of Cromford House and the best cook in the whole of Yorkshire." He gave her a wide beaming grin. Janice broke into a peal of laughter. "Get away with you," and gave Mr Walker a playful nudge, her face flushed pink with delight at the compliment.

I stood up from stroking the dog, which she seemed not to notice had disobeyed her orders and took my hands in hers. "Oh, hands as cold as ice!" she exclaimed. "Nice to meet you, love."

She had a pleasant face that was very smooth and shiny across her cheek bones and nose, but deep long lines radiated around her dark, almost black deep-set eyes. Brown age spots dotted the back of her soft smooth hands, while several nestled on her forehead and flushed cheeks. I had always thought how strange it was that these marks were looked on with such scorn. The way they were despised as though they were some sort of badge of old age. I had always found them to look quite beautiful on most of the older women I had seen. Rather like knots in silken polished wood. However, I was only twenty-six so maybe in another forty or so years I would change my view. Age spots or not, Janice had a pretty face and intelligent eyes, and she fixed those eyes on me now. She looked rather like a blackbird in appearance, plump, small, and rounded with bright eyes. She cocked her head to one side ever so slightly emphasising the image in my mind while she studied me like I was some fat juicy worm there for the taking. "Well," she said at length, "can't say I see much of a family resemblance. Are you sure she's a Cromford?" she said to Mr Walker.

He just smiled and nodded.

I didn't take any offence at what she said. It was just a simple statement of fact and had been said with no malicious intent.

"Mrs Maxwell at home?" Peter asked.

"Yes." She turned her gaze back to me. "She really is eager to meet you. In fact, to tell the truth we all have," she blushed again. "I'll take you through."

"It's all right, Janice," said Mr Walker gently taking my hands from her grip. "I'll take Emily through."

She looked a little put out but shrugged it off saying lightly with a smile, "I expect you'll want a pot of tea bringing through" and then winking at Mr Walker, "and a few biscuits."

Janice now turned her attention to the Labrador that was busy sniffing at my feet while the little spaniel had also crept silently back to see who was here. She looked down sharply, "Charlie-boy," she said in a crisp tone. At this the spaniel rolled over on to its back and looked up at her with the most appealing chocolate brown eyes.

Janice sniffed. "He's a pest that one. Been under my feet all morning. What he needs is a good walk." At the mention of the word walk the spaniel leapt up and both dogs went charging off in the direction of what I presumed to be the kitchen. Janice shook her head.

"Mrs Maxwell is in the front room. I'll get someone to deal with the dogs." Janice turned and headed off in the same direction of the dogs. "Simon!" she called out. "I want those dogs out of my kitchen."

I followed Mr Walker to a door on the opposite side of the staircase from where Janice had disappeared. He gave it a light tap and then softly opened the door.

We entered a light airy room that was flooded with sunshine. Along one wall were several French windows that opened out onto the top terrace of the house. On the opposite wall there was a large fireplace and like the hallway there was a log fire glowing in the hearth. Another black labrador was stretched out on the rug in front of the fire, but unlike the other two boisterous dogs that I'd just encountered, this dog showed no signs of getting up to greet me. Instead, it lay heavily on its side, its thick black tail beating rhythmically on the rug.

There was a variety of sofas and easy chairs in the room, and in the far corner by one of the French windows was a piano and to the side of that there was a small circular table that had a glass vase stood on it that was filled with yellow and white freesia. I could smell their perfume and I closed my eyes breathing in their sweet smell for a moment lost in my secret flower-filled world.

It was a lovely room, full of character and charm; nothing seemed to match but went together perfectly.

In a chair close to the fire there was an elegant looking woman who had been reading a book. On entering the room, she had looked up and carefully placed her bookmark at the page she had been reading and placed it on a small table beside her. She took her reading glasses off and placed them on top of her book and then gracefully walked over to greet us.

She appeared to be in her mid-fifties, but I knew from what Mr walker had told me that she must be at least ten years older. Her hair was a beautiful, muted shade of gold. Time it seemed had only robbed it of its former depth and vitality. She wore it swept up off her face, which accentuated her high cheekbones and almond shaped eyes. She had the same elegance of bearing that I had seen in the photograph of my father, and she also had his stature.

"Peter, how lovely to see you." she said in a smooth velvet-like voice. She stretched out her graceful arms in greeting and kissed Mr Walker gently on the cheek and then turned towards me.

"Emily?" she asked taking both my hands in hers which were warm and smooth. She looked at me closely with the most remarkable jade green eyes. If she thought the same as Janice about my looks, she kept it to herself.

"Charming, quite charming," she said softly. "Now come and sit down and tell me all about yourself."

"Well, I'll leave you two ladies to get acquainted."

"Yes that's a good idea, thank you. Raymond and Miranda are in the office I expect that there are things you need to discuss." Lillian Maxwell said.

Mr Walker smiled, nodded then left the room, closing the door behind him.

Lillian and I talked for almost three hours. So engrossed where we in our conversation that we forgot lunch. Janice, worried that we would starve, crept in with tea and sandwiches, muttering something about food going cold and plates of wasted food.

I told Lillian of my childhood and of the flower shop and about my home and my hobby painting. She thought that it was interesting that I had such a passion for flowers as both her mother and grandfather had been such keen gardeners. She told me how the garden around the house had been landscaped by them and that they were now open to the public on occasional weekends and bank holidays.

We talked at length about her mother, my mother and of her daughter Miranda and of course about Cromford House, the estate and the business.

"You know it's so very odd," she said, "but I can never recall my mother ever mentioning a brother." She got up and threw another log on the fire. Duchess (for I had been told that was the name of the dog) stirred a little and rolled over to toast her little round belly.

Realizing that I might misinterpret this comment as though she was questioning my identity she added quickly, "Oh, I mean I am sure she had a brother, but to never mention him I find that very strange, don't you?"

She came to sit beside me again. She looked at me, puzzlement clouding her eyes. "I have looked through every photograph album in the house trying to find some picture of someone who might have been him. I have spent days in the attic going through boxes of stuff trying to find at least some reference or connection, but nothing; not one single thing." She sighed, "I even went through mum's old letters and diaries. I felt dreadful doing so and it was all for nothing. Not one reference, not one. It's as though his entire existence and connection to this family has been ..." she groped for the word.

"Erased," I offered.

"Yes, that's it: Erased, totally wiped out from existence and with an almost surgical precision, too!"

"Why?" I said in a small, bewildered voice. it was a question that I was asking myself and I did not expect an answer from Lillian, for I knew she was just as perplexed as I.

Why had Edward Cromford been so effectively removed from the family history and for what purpose, and perhaps more worryingly, just what he had done to warrant such extreme measures. Then, strangely after decades of denial to be re-introduced to the family in what can only be described as a theatrical manner. I could only conclude that there was something rather sinister about Edward Cromford, the thought was rather a worrying one: just how many skeletons were in the cupboard.

I believe that Lillian and I were sharing the same thought, because we both sat in silence listening to the logs crackle on the fire and Duchess softly snoring, both too afraid to voice our fears and both fearing the worst.

"Oh heavens!" she suddenly cried out aloud waking Duchess up mid snore with a startled half-hearted bark.

"The will is to be read very soon and I haven't shown you to your room. How selfish of me, you must want to freshen up!"

My room was decorated in shades of lavender and primrose and the furniture was white lacquered wood, a little in the style of French regency, but without all the opulent gilding. The soft furnishings were very Laura Ashley in design and gave the room a lovely country style charm. It was all very feminine, and I adored it.

My suitcase had been brought in from the car and had been left at the foot of the bed. Lilian told me that she would come back for me in half an hour and take me down to the office boardroom where the will was to be read.

"Emily," she said pausing in the doorway, "I'm so glad that you came. I want you to feel that Cromford House is your home, and you treat it as such." Still smiling, she turned and left the room closing the door behind her.

I ignored my suitcase and wandered over to the window. My room was at the front of the house, and I was treated once more to the view of the dale and gardens. The sky had now clouded over softly diffusing the view. It still looked very cold outside and the mist that was slowly rising from the river was thick and heavy, laden with frost. I had a much better view of the front garden from this angle, and I could see just how steep a slope it was built on.

There were four wide terraces that had been built to compensate for the incline and they were deep as a series of steps interlinked them.

Much of the snow and ice had melted in the earlier sunshine and I could see that the upper terrace had been laid out with formal beds and there was a large ornamental pond in the centre. This was the terrace that the French doors of the sitting room where I had been with Lillian would open out onto and I thought how delightful it was. The other terraces were laid out with a similar theme but without ponds. The last terrace took you out onto a long sweeping lawn that had two parallel borders on either side of the terrace steps, and a central grass path that beckoned the traveller along its length and down towards an orchard and then the river and woods beyond. The borders seemed to be quite empty, but I guessed they were full of sleeping plants and I imagined towering delphiniums, scarlet poppies, and brazen oxeye daisies. In summer they would be a feast of colour and sound, with buzzing bees and beautiful flamboyant butterflies. Even now I thought if I were to take a closer look, I would most likely find clumps of snowdrops and maybe dusky pink or creamy white hellebores, perhaps winter heathers and the sharp green spears of daffodil leaves poking through the soil. As beautiful as this scene was and the pictures of the flowers that I created in my mind it was the high moorland that really dominated this landscape.

I could see the start of the moorland stretching up to the left of the window where I was standing, and I knew from the approach to the house it extended up further and wrapped itself around the house. I shivered, not because I was cold but because the barrenness of the moor both frightened me and intrigued me. I had a sudden longing to leave the warmth and security of the house and walk on that moor, filling my lungs with the cold air and feeling the emptiness around me. I was enchanted by its mystical beauty and by its power. Lillian's words came back to me: yes, I would very much like to feel that this could be home to me. Yet in less than an hour's time those words spoken with such sincerity would come back at me with a savage vengeance that would rip my world apart and a those around me.

Chapter four

We assembled for the reading of the will in a small boardroom towards the back of the house. The room was brightly lit and warm, the heat coming from a radiator rather than an open fire. An assortment of framed certificates hung on one wall and the only furniture in the room other than the oval polished table where we sat, was a wooden sideboard in the same medium oak colour as the table. This was completely bare except for a silver tray that had half a dozen crystal tumblers and a decanter that was filled with an amber coloured liquid.

Mr Walker sat at the head of the table and wore an uncharacteristic sombre expression. I sat on his left with my back to the window and Lillian sat next to me.

Opposite was Janice who looked terrified, and Raymond Maxwell sat next to her. He was a well-built muscular man, who had a weathered craggy face that resembled a chewed butterscotch toffee. His hair was graphite grey with a thick wiry texture that showed no sign of thinning. He wore a dark navy-blue suit but underneath the jacket he wore a green checked shirt of brushed cotton. He kept fiddling with his tie in an impatient, irritable manner, and I wondered if Lillian had told him to wear a suit today because he looked like a little boy who had been forced into an uncomfortable sailor's outfit for a cousin's wedding.

As he slid a stout finger under the collar of his shirt for the third time and threw Lillian a surreptitious look of annoyance, I smiled across at him. He grinned back with small square set teeth.

Sitting next to Raymond was the most extraordinary, beautiful woman. She had the same delicate bone structure and almond shaped eyes as Lillian and appeared to be in her early thirties. This must be Lillian's daughter Miranda I thought.

Her hair was cut into a chin length bob and was a pale blonde – like the colour of champagne. She had a full, blunt cut fringe with a centre parting that framed her lovely face and provided the perfect setting for her light sky blue eyes. She was as slender and as graceful as her mother, but unlike Lillian who exuded a natural glowing warmth. There was nothing warm about Miranda Maxwell. She was as cold as polished steel.

Mr Walker perched a pair of reading glasses on the end of his nose and cleared his throat looking at each of us individually, signalling that he was about to start. Lillian took hold of my hand under the table and gave it a little squeeze. I was glad of the gesture, although I was sure it was as much for her sake as mine.

"Thank you for coming," Mr Walker began.

It took only ten minutes to read the will and then what seemed like a lifetime that we all sat in stunned silence all opened mouthed and gawping at each other in disbelief. It was Raymond who broke the silence. "Lillian!" he roared. "Did you know about this?"

I felt her grip tighten on my hand. "No! Of course not," she said indignantly in a controlled if slightly higher pitched voice than normal.

"I'll contest it," Raymond shouted, swinging his gaze from Lillian to glare at Peter Walker.

"I'll bloody well contest it. Roberta must have lost her marbles."

Mr Walker who remained seated and composed tried to speak, but Raymond suddenly got up so violently that his chair toppled over. I was now the object of his fury, his eyes were black with rage and sunk back into his face, his features twisted and distorted with rage in a flushed red face. "And you," he bellowed pointing towards me with his finger stabbing wildly at the air with each syllable he spoke. "Are a fraudster."

He smashed his clenched fist onto the table, turned and kicked the fallen chair out of his way as he strode towards the door, then left the room slamming the door so violently that one of the pictures fell to the floor with a shattering noise that sent shards of broken glass across the oatmeal carpet.

Lillian let go of my hand. Her face was white and set with anger. She rose and left the room with a sweeping graceful movement.

However, Lillian was not fleeing, nor was her anger directed at me, she had gone in search of her husband.

Janice jumped up, seeing this as her opportunity to escape the room. "I'll fetch a dustpan and brush," she said.

How I also longed to escape from that room. Suddenly it seemed far too hot and stuffy. The cloying atmosphere was making me feel ill. I needed some fresh air and time to think. I needed to be alone and have space to breathe. I felt physically sick, my heart was pounding so loudly that I was afraid I would choke. The room started to fade. My head became fuzzy, and my mouth went dry.

Miranda spoke. Her voice smooth and cold like ice, metaphorically slapping me across the face and bringing me back to my senses with an abrupt jolt.

"If I am to understand correctly," she said in a voice that betrayed not one single trace of emotion, "my grandmother has left the house and grounds and a share of the estate to Miss Cromford because she believed that her brother should have been the one to inherit and not herself when their father died?"

Mr Walker nodded. "Yes, in essence. It troubled your grandmother greatly that her brother had been excluded."

"And it took her over sixty years to ease that guilt?" Miranda said.

"I don't know why it took her so long or the reason why," Mr Walker continued. "But I do know that she wanted to set things straight and she wanted above all else to make sure she was being fair."

"Fair? I really don't see anything fair about it. My father and I have worked hard at maintaining the estate and we have made a very profitable business from it. Cromford House is also my home."

"And you will continue to run the business and live at Cromford House should you wish to do so. There are provisions in the will to ensure this," Mr Walker calmly stated.

"Oh yes." Miranda raised a quizzical elegant eyebrow, "like the provision that the first-born grandchild will be the next in line to inherit! A little old fashioned and outdated don't you think? And that assumes of course there will be grandchildren."

"Perhaps, but I am only acting out with accordance with her wishes. And I believe that you, Miranda should respect those wishes."

Miranda's face flushed a delicate shade of pink. "Yes," she quietly mumbled, but I couldn't tell if she was embarrassed or just annoyed. Mr Walker continued, "Your grandmother felt that it was very important that her brother, or at least his children, should he have had any," he paused and smiled at me. "Should have a share of the inheritance. And of course, there was a child, a grandchild."

"I see," said Miranda, "so if it had turned out that there had been no offspring then my mother or I would have been the sole beneficiaries?"

Mr Walker nodded, as a slight frown crossed Miranda's otherwise serene face before she thoughtfully said, "And if Emily were ... to die."

I felt myself sit bolt upright as though a cold iron rod had been inserted down the length of my spine. An ice-like chill was paralysing me. I have often heard the expression of blood running cold but never thought that it actually could. Yet under Miranda's unwavering blue eyes and a statement that she said so casually my blood did indeed run cold.

"Forgive me." She smiled in my direction, but there was no warmth in that lovely face, despite the faint flush of colour that had risen once again to her cheeks. "Of course, I don't mean ..." She faulted acutely aware now of her faux pas. "What I mean to say is ... I just want to understand the terms of the will better."

Mr Walker sighed and sat back in his chair studying Miranda thoughtfully for a few moments and then answered her in a matter-of-fact tone.

"If Miss Cromford were to die leaving no child of her own and presuming you had a child then your child would be the one to inherit."

"And if there were no children?" she questioned.

"Then I would strongly recommend that Miss Cromford make a will of her own."

She nodded her head softly in acknowledgement then apologised, but that apology was not out of any sympathy for me but for the shame she had brought on herself.

Mr Walker nodded his head in acknowledgment and spoke. "I discussed the will with your grandmother at great length Miss Maxwell. She was very concerned that it would cause you distress, but she was convinced that it was the right thing to do. She has left you with substantial gifts and you are of course free to do whatever you wish with these. But the house and grounds will belong to Miss Cromford as per your grandmother's wishes.

"So, contesting it will be useless?"

"Yes, she was of sound mind when the will was written, of that I have no doubt."

She bowed her head in silent acceptance and got up to leave, when she paused and turned around from the door, one hand delicately poised on the shiny brass knob. "But Emily could sell the house if she wished too." she faltered, not quite sure how to continue without offending Mr Walker, because I was quite sure that she had no consideration for my feelings. "And her share in the estate should she wish?"

"She could, but of course it would be very difficult for her to get a buyer. You and your parents are sitting tenants and you and your father have total control over the business and estate. The first-born child will be the next to inherit. So, in effect Emily is just a custodian; she really has nothing of any value to sell. Unless you would like to make her an offer?"

Miranda thought for a moment then shook her head leaving the room silently leaving a faint but delicious smell of jasmine in the air.

When at last Mr Walker and myself were alone I whispered in a hoarse voice that I barely recognized as my own," you said no more surprises."

"Yes, "he said." but in my defence I did say for the moment."

"That's a poor excuse," I snapped back.

"Yes, your right it is." He looked apologetically at me.

"I mean, could you have least hinted - something – anything except this farce?"

"I am so very sorry Emily. You can now see how delicate this whole situation was. And as I have mentioned before I'm also legally bound.

"Well, Roberta should have told everyone of her intention – or didn't she care either?" My anger was now surfacing, and I began to raise my voice.

"She died before she had the chance to," he said quietly.

"Oh," I said. I was beginning to regret my hasty words.

He got up and wandered over to the sideboard. Tracing a finger along the smooth shiny surface. He spoke very quietly, his voice nothing more than a whisper.

"I told you how she came to see me to change the will, but what I didn't tell you was that I recommended against it. I thought that leaving a legacy of this size to what amounts to a total stranger foolish, but she was adamant. And she was certainly of sound mind so I agreed, but there are certain terms and conditions within the will that I suggested were added that would protect the house and estate, and of course the rest of the family."

"You mean like that it would be difficult for me to sell?"

"Yes. And of course, to ensure that the house stays within the family it passes to the next born child. Assuming of course there is one."

He turned to face me again. He suddenly looked very old. And so very tired. "I read the will today in the manner that I thought best. All beneficiaries were seated together so everyone knew together. I knew it would be explosive, and hurtful to Miranda, but I have a job to do and above all else I needed to honour Mrs Cromford and her final wishes."

I nodded. "I just wish that you had given me some clue."

He sighed. "I know. There are still several details that we need to finalise. Would you be able to stay on for a couple of extra days before returning to Swansea?"

I faulted. "I don't know. I expect so, but where do you mean, here at Cromford House?"

"Well, yes, of course. The house after all is yours now."

I was glad when I finally left that room. It wasn't yet quite dark outside so on impulse I pulled on my coat and woollen hat and walked out into the cold evening air thrusting my hands deep into my pockets.

How cool and refreshing the air was on my face and I wandered down the steps of the upper terrace not really knowing where I was going or caring. A blackbird rushed out of some dense shrubs making me start. It flew out in front of me, screeching its indignation at having been disturbed.

I almost ran down the two next flight of steps and then realising that I had nowhere to go I sank down onto a nearby bench in defeat.

The snow and ice had almost all but melted away and now there was a delicate mist that was swirling and rising from the river, creeping across the woods, and stretched -out lawns. Tiny pin pricks of light penetrated the swelling gloom as streetlights began to flicker on heralding the coming of night. I sat still and watched the light fade and welcomed the shroud of darkness as it stealthily crept around me.

Out of the corner of my eye a sudden movement made me quickly turn my head and, in the gloom, I could just make out the shape of the two dogs. one small with floppy ears ambling along and the other large and clumsy, running about. They were the two dogs that I had seen earlier in the day and following on behind there appeared to be a man. At first, I thought it was Raymond and I felt myself shrink back into the shadows. But as he got closer, I could see that this was a much younger and taller man with a long powerful stride. Spiralling wisps of steam swirled around them like dragon's breath, and I wondered if I could just slink away into a nearby love arbour before I was seen when he raised his hand in greeting and called out "hello."

Realizing now that I would be obliged to stay where I was, I shouted a half-hearted "hello" back.

As he got closer, I could see that his red hair, a deep coppery colour was cut close to his head but curling in the nape of his neck and around his ears. He had the same coppery stubble on his cheeks and chin and when he smiled at me, he revealed deep long dimples on each of his cheeks – they looked like lichen-covered crags. "It's a bit cold to be sitting out here." he said smiling down at me.

He paused for a moment waiting for me to respond but I said nothing, so he sat down beside me on the bench. "You must be the infamous Emily Cromford."

I looked at him sharply

"Janice," he stated.

"Oh."

"Fastest form of communication known to humankind is Janice. I expect the whole dale will know by now."

I didn't know whether to laugh or cry at this statement. I heard myself give a deep groan out loud and continued to sit in silence.

"Look it really is too cold to be sitting out here. Let me walk you back to the house," he said in a matter of fact take charge tone of voice.

There seemed little point in arguing with him, and he was right it was far too cold to be sitting outside on a cold damp bench in the dark.

He whistled to the dogs, and they came along bounding up behind us, following him obediently as we walked back toward the house.

"Was it really bad?" he asked.

"It was bad," I replied.

He was quiet for a moment and then said, "Raymond's bark is far worse than his bite. I should know I have been on the receiving end on many occasions." He grinned opening the front door of the house for me. The dogs suddenly overtook us and came barging past us almost knocking me off balance as they charged through the door of the house. He muttered something under his breath after them as I watched them disappear down the hall leaving a trail of muddy pawprints in their wake. "Janice won't be too happy about that," he commented. "Should have used the side door, never mind too late now." he shrugged.

"You should be thrilled you know," he motioned with his head toward the house, "to have all this left to you. It's one hell of a legacy. By the way," he said casually with a grin that made his deep brown eyes sparkle like newly shelled conkers, "I'm Simon – Simon Taylor … head game keeper and loyal employee at your service."

I didn't go down to dinner that evening. I acted like a coward and stayed within the sanctuary of my own room. I knew that I would have to face everyone sooner or later, but later was my preferred option at the moment. I had told mum that I would ring that evening, but I even shied away from that prospect, fearing that on hearing her bright aminated and cheerful voice that my own would crack and I was loath to burden her with my misery. How I despised myself for shutting myself away and acting like a fool.

There came a light tapping at the door.

"Yes," I called out walking toward the door.

"It's me, Lillian. can I come in?"

I opened the door, avoiding eye contact. She carried a tray with a bowl of hot steaming soup and some crusty bread rolls.

"I thought you might be hungry," she smiled shyly at me.

I felt so foolish and ashamed. "I am so sorry "I began my voice trembling a little." Lillian set the tray down on a small table in my room and then turned towards me.

"Whatever do you have to be sorry about?"

"Everything … tonight … Dinner … This afternoon," my voice trailed away, as it began to quake.

"Nonsense," she said in a matter-of-fact tone "you have absolutely nothing to be sorry about. If anyone should be apologising, it should be Raymond."

I lifted my head and my eyes met hers which were bright and shining and had a look of defiance about them. "Here drink this. "She handed me a glass tumbler of pale gold liquid, "it will make you feel better."

She handed me the glass and I sniffed the contents. Whiskey. I hated whiskey. It smelt vile and made me wrinkle my nose up in disgust. Oh, what the hell I thought and took a large gulp.

It was repugnant. Its foul bitter taste filled my mouth and made me want to wretch. I swallowed it quickly, anxious to rid myself of the taste and smell of it. It glided down my throat like smooth velvet, leaving a trail of warmth in its wake that spread through my chest before fanning out and caressing my stomach with heated tendrils. It felt good, really good.

"Now," said Lillian in a motherly voice, "you have nothing to be sorry about."

"But ..."

"No buts, I have spoken with Peter and although I admit I am shocked at my mother's wishes I can't say that I am surprised. I know that what she has done was with the best intentions, I just wish that she had had the time to tell us first! Anyway, what is done is done and I for one intend to respect her wishes."

"And Raymond?"

"Oh, Raymond." She waved her hand dismissively in the air, "will have to like it or lump it!"

She smiled at me taking my hand in hers and looked deep into my eyes. "Don't worry Emily, by tomorrow Raymond will have calmed down, he's just a big pussy cat, you'll see. Now you finish off that whiskey and eat your soup while it's still hot and then get a good night's sleep."

"Thank you, Lillian," I said touched by her sincere kindness. She leaned towards me and kissed my forehead. "Goodnight, Emily, everything will be all right. I promise."

When she had gone, I ate the soup and finished my drink then sank down onto the bed when the tears finally came. Hot, salty tears that stung my eyes and burned my cheeks. I buried my face in my pillow and sobbed like a child, each breath wracking my body until at last I had no strength left and I gratefully succumbed to sleep.

Chapter five

The next few days passed quickly and most of my time was spent holed up in an office with Miranda going over tedious amounts of paperwork. My relationship with Raymond had improved dramatically. His apology to me about his conduct at the will reading was heartfelt and genuine. He was embarrassed and regretted his hasty words. I discovered that Raymond's fiery temper was off- set by a generous warm heart.

My relationship with Miranda however had not improved. Each day I was greeted with her cool blue eyes and a frosted smile. Her politeness to me was impeccable, but there was never any hint of sincerity in the conversations we had together.

Peter Walker sometimes came briefly to our meetings. I was always grateful when he did as he managed to lighten the mood between Miranda and myself. Through these meetings I was told about the running of the estate, the many aspects of the business and the running of the house. My head began to swim with all the information that I was been imparted with. I understood very little of it and if I am being honest, I found quite dull.

Miranda passed me yet another sheet of paper. "These are all our employees."

I glanced down at the list and saw Simon's name. "I've met Simon."

"Oh ... you have?" she looked a little taken aback. "When was this?"

"The day of my arrival. I was out in the garden, and he had just returned from a walk with the dogs."

"I see." She studied me thoughtfully for longer than I felt necessary then said, "Well Simon is our head gamekeeper. Did he mention this?"

"Yes, he did as a matter of fact." We were playing a strange game of cat and mouse, and I did not intend on being the mouse.

"Yes, of course he did, "she muttered to herself with a slight trace of annoyance. "Well," she continued in her refined cool voice, "Simon oversees the other keepers and the moorland for the shooting: the grouse and pheasant. He also aids with the river management. We lease off stretches of the river and we have the large fishponds for anglers. There is a private stretch of river at the end of the garden that my grandmother liked to fish. Do you fish Miss Cromford?"

"No." I said, noting the use of my name – Miss Cromford, not Emily. "I don't shoot either," I added.

"Do you not approve of these activities?"

I faltered; I did not want to be drawn into a discussion that I knew nothing about. Miranda's image of me was of a city dweller who had no right to be here in what she saw as her domain. She knew that I was uncomfortable in these unfamiliar surroundings, and she was making every effort to make me feel like a fool.

"I neither approve nor disapprove," I said calmly and then added, "I have no intention of interfering with the business Miranda; and any way I don't believe that I could even if I wanted to."

"No, you can't. I just wanted to make sure that you clearly understood that point." And with that she continued to discuss the various business activities.

The day before I was due to return home to Swansea, Miranda told me that she had a prior engagement and that as far as she was concerned our meetings had concluded. I was delighted. I saw this as a chance to escape the confines of the house and to explore the garden.

The weather had turned milder during the last couple of days, for most of the time it had rained. It had fallen from dull dark skies, and a thick mist had obscured the dale and moor. Today a breeze had risen and cleared away the clouds and mist and the sun put in a welcome appearance every now and then. There was still the threat of rain as every so often we were given a sharp heavy shower but overall, it was dry.

I borrowed one of the many waterproof coats that was hanging in the hallway and rummaged about until I found a suitable pair of boots that fitted me. I pulled on my gloves and found a bright red bobble hat in one of the baskets in the hallway. The overall effect wasn't exactly flattering or stylish, but it would keep me both warm and dry.

Duchess watched me expectantly, tail wagging gently and soft chocolate brown eyes looking at me pleadingly. Duchess seemed to have taken a bit of a shine to me as she always seemed to be by my side. I admit that in the last few days I had grown quite fond of her too and I was glad of her company and the comradeship.

"Come on then," I said as I opened the front door and stepped out into the cool morning air. I breathed in the fresh air rather like a prisoner who had been released from the confines of a cell. I could feel the claustrophobia of the past few days leave my body. There was a strong cold wind that was pushing dark clouds across an unsettled sky. Every so often the sun would appear, briefly illuminate everything in a triumphant wave of gold and colourful rainbows and then a cloud would cross its face and snatch it back it again, glaring menacingly over the dale with the threat of rain or hail.

I wandered over to an ornamental circular pond that was in the middle of the upper terrace. In the centre was a stone mermaid. She was raised on a pedestal and seemed to float above the water, her hands were outstretched and cupped together with water trickling over them and through her fingers splashing gently into the pool below.

Several koi carp of a medium size sulked about by the baskets at the bottom of the pond. The lily leaves were no more than snake-like stems, withered and brown waiting patiently for the spring sunshine to bring them back to life. The wind was quite bitter, so I followed the steps down to the next terrace which would provide a little more shelter.

Set into the wall of this terrace was a stone head of a lion. Water was trickling from its mouth and running into a trough below which duchess was now noisily slurping from.

Two wooden benches were on either side of the trough and the walls were covered with the stems of climbing plants, roses, and honeysuckle. There was also a winter flowering clematis. Its bell-shaped flowers were a delicate shade of cream with pale pink splodges randomly scattered over the petals and it had the most delicate fern like leaves, deeply forked and a dark, almost black like green. The flowers swayed in the breeze, and I found myself taking a step closer and examining them. They had a delicious, sweet smell.

I turned from the clematis and began to walk down the next flight of steps that would take me to the next terrace. It led me to several long and deep flower beds that ran the length of the terrace, and I wandered slowly along admiring the garden and the view of the dale. The earth was dark and crumbly having been recently forked over. The emerald spears of daffodil shoots pierced the soil at intervals and ranks of white pansies lined the front of the beds. Drifts of snowdrops, and dusky pink Lenten roses nodded their heads rhythmically in the wind as though dancing to a magical orchestra that only they could hear.

Duchess followed on behind, stopping to sniff at things on the way but never more than a few paces behind me. I went down another flight of steps still anxious to get out of the biting wind.

This had its high walls covered in rose stems. All neatly pruned and tied into horizontal wires that were evenly spaced out on the wall. Small crimson buds were visible on the stems and in a few weeks' time these would be bursting into tiny, freshly formed leaves, the colour of pomegranate seeds.

There were no long formal flower beds on this level as it had been laid out in the style of an Elizabethan knot garden. Each geometric bed had been edged with lavender or box. Gravel paths ran between the beds and each bed was filled with rose bushes; bare branched and sleeping. This was very much a sheltered part of the garden as at last I had found shelter from the wind. The sun had once more won the upper hand in its battle and for the moment shone brightly. I closed my eyes and held my face up to its warmth, letting it caress my skin while I imagined the heady scent of roses and lavender on a warm summer's evening.

"Sorry Miss – gardens aren't open today."

Startled I opened my eyes and abruptly spun round to see a man coming towards me with a wheelbarrow. He had fair, floppy hair that touched his shoulders and partially covered his eyes. He wore a thick navy woollen sweater and faded light blue jeans that were tucked into a pair of wellington boots. "Weekends and bank holidays. It says so on the gates at the bottom."

He set down the barrow and walked towards me, pushing his hair from his face in an absent-minded manner.

"Oh," I began.

He caught sight of Duchess who was ambling along the gravel path behind me. I could see a faint flush of colour creep up his neck. "I'm sorry" he mumbled, "I thought you were a visitor."

To save him any more discomfort I shrugged and took off my glove and held out my hand towards him. "Emily Cromford."

He glanced down at his hands, which were grubby with soil and hastily wiped them on the legs of his jeans. "Robin," he said shaking my hand.

His hands were warm and dry and a little rough. "Nice to meet you, Robin."

He bent down to pat Duchess who was now eagerly sniffing his boots and wagging her tail, giving me the opportunity to observe him more closely without being obvious.

He was of a similar age to me, maybe a year or two older and he was slimly built with a strong angular body and of an average height. His nose was just ever so slightly crooked, perhaps the result of it being broken in the past, and his lashes were thick and of a sandy colour. He looked up and I saw that his eyes were a deep grey green – they reminded me of wet slate, sparkling in the sunshine.

I would not describe him as a handsome man, but he was attractive in a pleasant, charming sort of way. Surreptitiously I slid my bobble hat off and tried unsuccessfully to stuff it in my coat pocket and said flippantly, "I thought everyone would know who I was by now."

"I heard, but you're not what I was expecting."

"Oh, and what did you expect?"

He paused for a minute, and then said very seriously, "A crusty old trout of a woman."

He smiled making his eyes crinkle and sparkle. I laughed.

"What do you think of the gardens?" he asked.

"I haven't had much of a chance to explore them, and the weather has been appalling since my arrival."

"Weather's always like this," he teased. "But if you have time now, I can take you on a guided tour."

I nodded; I really could not think of anything more pleasant than walking around the garden in his company.

I called to Duchess who followed us down onto the last terrace and then out onto the wide sweeping lawn that I had seen from my bedroom window.

Robin talked about the garden with enthusiasm and affection. We chatted about the flowers, and I was soon enchanted not just with the garden but by Robin himself.

The well-tended lawn started to merge with a small meadow, there was a grassed path that led down through the meadow and another that crossed it horizontally.

"The orchards are down that path." Robin nodded his head towards the path that was straight in front of us. "And they lead down to the woods and the river. There's a summer house set down the end of the orchard. It's in a lovely spot but today we'll follow this other path that loops back towards the house." We began to follow the horizontal path.

Gradually we started to walk through a woodland of mainly deciduous trees; oak and sycamore for the most part and there were a few holly bushes that had still had some berries on. Young mountain ash and oak had been planted in small clearings. Their trunks were wrapped in a type of corrugated plastic. "Do you also tend to the woodland here?" I asked.

"Yes, it's all part of the grounds. We wrap the saplings like that to give them protection from the rabbits and the deer."

"You get deer in the woodland. Are they wild?"

"Yes," he smiled. "There's a surprisingly large population although you wouldn't know it. If you come out very early in the morning you are most likely to get a glimpse of one. Best leave the dog at home though."

The path started to become steeper and through the trees I could see that we were now level with the lower terraces, as we continued to walk until we passed the house and were above it on the hill side. The trees thinned out and we were greeted with a beautiful panoramic viewpoint and a bench to sit on.

"Wow, that's worth the climb," I breathed taking in the view. "I thought it was wonderful from the house, but from here you have a much better view of the moor."

He smiled. "I never tire of it. Of course, we also get a lot of fog and rain on account of being so high up on the moor. so, you don't always get to see it, but it's a real treat when you do."

I got my breath back from the steep climb and then we continued upwards for a short time. The path began to level out a little as we approached a rocky hill side. The site had been partially excavated. Holes had been dug for what looked to be several interlinking ponds on different levels and were connected with would be waterfalls.

"Work in progress," he said. "But I don't know if it'll get finished now."

"And why is that?" I asked.

He looked at me with a puzzled expression on his face. "Well, it's all down to you."

"Me! I don't understand."

"Well, you own the house and gardens. You hold the purse strings. When Mrs Cromford died all this was shelved and had to be left." He gestured with his hand towards the unfinished pond system. "If it hadn't been for Mrs Maxwell, I reckon we would have lost our jobs too."

"I see," I said, although I didn't. Had Miranda said anything about the gardens? I tried to think. Endless hours of tedious paperwork and being shut up in an office withering under her relentless, perfect gaze and I couldn't remember what she had said. I would have to risk her scorn and ask about the gardens at the earliest opportunity. It was not a conversation that I looked forward to.

I felt deflated. Had Robin only offered to give me a tour of the gardens to find out what my plans were and if his job was going to be safe?

"Have you worked here long?" I asked. He didn't seem to mind that I hadn't answered his question about the unfinished landscaping, because he just smiled and said." About six years."

"And you like it?"

He nodded. "Things haven't been too good since Mrs Cromford passed ... I mean," he floundered.

"it's ok," I said looking into his twinkling eyes.

We were both silent for a minute and I turned to gaze up at the moor that loomed above us on the hill side.

"This is all so strange," I whispered. "I just can't get used to the idea that all this is mine. How someone I never knew ... or met, could leave all this to me. It feels so unreal: so scary."

It was the first time that I told anyone how I really felt. Robin did not make me feel foolish like Miranda. Or ungrateful like Simon. Even Lilian for her kindness made me feel vulnerable and in need of protection. Robin just accepted my statement with a nod of his head.

We walked silently up the embankment on a partially marked out path which looped between the would-be ponds. I briefly paused at the top and looked down at the hillside. The earth lay in dark sodden clumps, half dug out with large rocks and boulders strewn about. Wooden stakes stuck out of the ground at intervals marking the different levels. For a moment, I shared Robin's vision of cool, running water cascading into deep pools with white water lilies and fern fronds. Stately candelabra primroses, yellow iris and purple loosestrife surrounding the ponds making them look as though they had been there forever and part of the natural landscape.

The sun disappeared behind a cloud again and my vision disappeared too, the lovely scene that I saw in my head had turned into the scarred and mutilated hillside that was reality.

We started to walk away, still in an upwards direction and as we rounded a final bend, I could see a large greenhouse and potting shed come into view.

"Headquarters!" Robin grinned.

Coming out of the potting shed was an older man. He wore a knitted multicolour sweater and a dark green padded body warmer; his trousers were also tucked into his wellington boots like Robin's were, and he had a cigarette dangling from his lower lip.

He looked up when he saw us and pushed the tweed cap he wore a little farther back on his head.

"Have you finished those roses yet lad?" he called out to Robin.

"Not yet. There's someone that I would like you to meet."

The man took a long drag on his cigarette, the smoke puffing about around him. Just then it started to rain. Great globes of freezing cold water fell from the sky with such force they stung your face. Duchess, with an uncharacteristic burst of speed went hurtling down the hill side towards the house. I could see that the back door in the courtyard was open and would take her through into the kitchen, I hoped that her paws weren't too muddy.

Just as suddenly the rain turned to hail. Robin grabbed my hand and together we made a dash for the greenhouse.

The air in the greenhouse was warm and humid but the noise was deafening. I feared that the hail would shatter the glass and for a minute or two I was genuinely frightened. The hail lessened and turned to rain once more.

Robin turned to me when at last we were able to speak above the clattering on the roof. "This is Tom," he said turning to introduce me to the man who had also followed us into the greenhouse.

"He's the one in charge around here."

"So, this is your girlfriend then?" he said to Robin with a sly grin.

"NO!" Robin and I chorused together.

"It's Miss Cromford you fool!" Robin corrected him, both of us blushing furiously. Tom pushed his cap further back on his head revealing a brown speckled head that looked like a newly laid hen's egg with strips of short white hair stuck around the sides.

"Ahh," the realisation sinking in. "She's not you girlfriend then. Pity!"

I shook Tom's outstretched hand and before I could stop myself, I said. "Oh freesias – they smell wonderful."

"We grow them for the house; they're one of Mrs Maxwell's favourite flowers." Robin said.

"We can grow pretty much anything you want," Tom boasted proudly. "There's another greenhouse a little further on behind this one as well."

The rain had receded to a gentle pitter-patter, and I began to walk along the flagged path of the greenhouse between the staging admiring the potted plants.

Here, at last, was something that I could identify with. I found the reassuring smell of the moist compost and plants and the gentle touch of the petals against my skin soothing. I listened to the gentle lullaby that was now being played by the rain on the roof and I breathed in the sweet damp smell of the earth. A tranquillity crept over me. Inevitably I began to arrange the flowers in my mind: Cineraria with its daisy like flowers edged in midnight blue and dazzling white centres, mixed with fragrant white jasmine and pale-yellow daffodils. The silvery stems of eucalyptus and the delicate nodding blooms of cape cowslip. I began to reel off the names of the plants as I passed them softly murmuring their names in Latin.

"You seem to know your stuff," said Tom surprised. "Have you had horticultural training?"

For a moment I had forgotten that I wasn't alone, and the sound of Tom's voice made me start. I turned to face Tom and Robin. "I work in a florist's shop." I felt so relaxed and content in the moist humid air of the greenhouse, filled with the plants and flowers that the tension of the last few days ebbed away, and I started to tell them about my job, the plans I had for the shop and this coming Valentine's Day. My obsession with flowers, my paintings and that one day I hoped to have a shop of my own, to design my own displays, and be my own boss. When just as suddenly I stopped. The realisation that all my plans that I had so carefully constructed for myself now looked uncertain. Roberta's will had changed everything.

"Well, that's just grand love," said Tom not sensing my sudden change of mood. "I have some seedlings to see to." He touched his cap and added, "Nice to meet you love." He turned and walked towards the door of the greenhouse. "Don't forget those roses lad," he called out to Robin before disappearing through the door.

"What's wrong?" Robin asked when Tom was out of earshot. I looked up at the roof of the greenhouse not really knowing what to say. I was unsure; I no longer knew where I was heading. I had lost my footing. I tried to speak, but the words wouldn't form. I was adrift in that cold lonely sea once more.

"You can't go back to your old life and you're afraid you won't fit in with this new one?" Robin whispered quietly.

I turned around so that I had my back to Robin and that he wouldn't be able to see the tears that were about to prick my eyes. I studied a pot of arum lilies, not yet in flower tracing the white spots on their sturdy leaves and slowly nodded, grateful that he understood without explanation.

Robin came to stand very close behind me. I could feel his warm breath and hear his gentle breathing. "You could still have your dream here if you wanted."

I sensed him reaching out almost touching my shoulder and then hesitate, not sure of my reaction. The moment passed and he said in a cheery bright voice. "Tour's over today. I really do have to get back to those roses."

I turned around to face him, the threat of tears gone and forced myself to smile at him. "Of course," I said, "and thank you for the tour." I also couldn't help but wonder what it would be like to kiss his soft pink lips.

Chapter six

The following day I was to leave for home. I had decided that I would return to Cromford House and live there, although I was unsure for how long this would be.

It had not been an easy decision. I would have to leave so much behind. Mum told me how she was looking forward to seeing Cromford House for herself and couldn't wait to visit, while Rita had said that she would take on a temporary assistant until I knew for sure what my future would be. I tried to convince myself that my hesitation was because of mum, despite her obvious excitement but I knew that the real reason was Miranda.

From our very first meeting she had intimidated me. I felt sure that her beautiful, polished exterior and icy aloofness hid a woman of deep passion. Whenever Miranda and I spoke, there was always an undercurrent, nothing you could quite pinpoint but there all the same. And the more time we spent in each other's company the more noticeable it became until it had evolved from a slight trace of annoyance to open dislike.

Despite all the problems that I faced living under the same roof as Miranda I wanted to stay if only for a short space of time. I felt that it was a connection with my father and grandfather. It was a new link, and I could not turn my back on it. So, I chose to stay, just as I knew my father would have done if he had been alive.

Lillian and Raymond were delighted with my decision, even Simon seemed pleased. Miranda said nothing, bowing her head silently in acknowledgment. On the morning of my departure, I was sitting at the breakfast table with Lillian and Miranda. Miranda was elegantly sipping coffee from a China cup when she looked up from the newspaper she was reading and spoke.

"Simon is unable to take you to the station this morning Emily. I have some important items that I need to go over with him."

"Can't it wait?" Lillian enquired.

"No, it can't," Miranda curtly replied.

I looked from mother to daughter. Lillian was studying Miranda closely, but even Lillian's shrewd eyes couldn't penetrate Miranda's outer shell. Lillian frowned while Miranda absorbed herself in folding the newspaper.

"Perhaps dad could take her? Or yourself?" Miranda suggested casually breaking the uncomfortable silence that had descended on the table.

"I don't want to be any trouble." I said quickly "I can get a taxi."

"Nonsense," Lillian sharply butted in, "Raymond can take you – if Simon's too busy that is."

This last part of the sentence was shot at Miranda with rapier like precision. "Anyway," Lillian said more agreeably, "I should like to come along too; Raymond and I can call in for lunch somewhere on the way back. I think I might even do a spot of shopping while in town."

To diffuse the tension between Miranda and Lillian, I decided that now was good a time as any to ask about the gardens. "I met a couple of the gardeners yesterday," I said brightly. One of them showed me the unfinished pond systems and asked if they were going to be completed."

"Did he?" Miranda said in an uninterested fashion.

"Yes, he was wondering if they were going to be completed now that the estate has been settled."

She turned her steady gaze to me. Her face beautifully made up, and her hair smooth and silky, perfectly styled, making me conscious of my own bare face still pink from the shower I had taken before breakfast and my damp hair that was now starting to curl around my face and shoulders. "The gardens are of no concern of mine. They were something of a hobby with my grandmother, you can do whatever you wish with them." She said.

So, this was what Robin had meant when he said it was down to me. He must have thought that I knew that the gardens were my sole responsibility. Lillian had been paying their wages from her own income, but I would, of course now be expected to pay them.

I sat back in my chair and took a sip of my tea thoughtfully. Roberta had ensured that I would have enough income to pay the household bills and a large sum of money for maintenance and repairs should it be needed, but this was all locked up in a trust fund. I would need to speak to Mr Walker. My outgoings were considerable, but now with the added expense of the gardens all my income would be swallowed up. Things were looking decidedly grim.

Raymond agreed to take me to the train station but raised his eyes to the ceiling making a tutting sound when Lillian suggested that they could do a little shopping together while in the town.

"All right," he reluctantly agreed. "But no shoe shops Lillian." He warned her.

"No shoe shops," she promised and winked at me.

Just as I was about to climb into the back of Raymond's range rover, Janice came rushing out of the house brandishing a thermos flask and large Tupperware box, thrusting them into my hand.

"Something for the journey."

I thanked her and looked down at the box which was crammed with sandwiches, cake, and fruit.

"You don't want to be eating all that pre-packed rubbish, and they know how to charge for it mind."

She then went on to tell me about a recent trip to Leeds to see her sister and the 'orribble tea that she got from the buffet trolley. "Gave it right back," she said. "I told him to put the bag back in and let it mash for a bit. And the cost, well I ask you, and all for a cup of hot water."

As we set off down the drive I waved goodbye to Janice, twisting my body round in the back seat as she stood on the steps of the house waving after us, Duchess looking sad and forlorn at my departure.

The trip into Skipton was very pleasant, Lillian and I chatting all the way. When we arrived at the station, I told them both that I would be fine, and they were to go off and enjoy themselves shopping. Raymond grunted at this sentiment and declared shopping was not his idea of fun and likened the whole experience to a trip to the dentist.

To occupy myself on the long journey home I bought myself a couple of magazines from the newspaper stand, and as I was paying for them, I heard the echoing tones of the announcement for my train arriving.

I made my way along the platform. Struggling with my case, handbag, and a family sized picnic box. I shoved the thermos further under my arm which held enough tea to quench the thirst of fifteen workmen, as I struggled to keep my balance. I wobbled this way and that, toppling over every so often and muttering my apologies to people as I bumped into them. From out of nowhere a pair of hands swooped down and took my bags: it was Robin.

"What are you doing here?" I gasped, as we continued walking towards my train.

Robin seemed to have little trouble navigating his way along the busy platform nimbly moving out of the way of the other passengers.

"I had to come into town today. I've just seen Mr and Mrs Maxwell. Mr Maxwell was muttering something about shoes? Anyway, they told me they had just dropped you off. I thought you might need a hand."

We arrived at my train and Robin helped me on board with my luggage. He looked at the thermos and box of food in my hands.

"From Janice?" he grinned.

"From Janice!" I nodded, and we both laughed.

"When are you coming back" he asked.

"As soon as I have things settled at home. I don't know maybe next month."

"Do you want to?"

"What, leave home?"

"No, come back?"

We were being jostled by people either boarding or leaving the train.

There was another call for my train announcing its departure. "I have to go," I said. "But yes, I do want to come back."

I turned and left him to board the train making my way towards a window seat. When I had finally arranged myself, I scanned the crowd that was milling about eagerly searching for a slimly built man with shaggy fair hair, but with a sigh of disappointment I realised he had gone.

The journey home was as tedious as I had expected. Once in Leeds I had to change trains. There were of course all the inevitable delays, late trains, faulty points, and engine trouble, and it was almost midnight when my taxi pulled up outside my home. I was cold, hungry, and exhausted. I had finished off the last of the sandwiches somewhere near Bristol and drained the last of the tea on the outskirts of Cardiff. Thank heavens I thought for Janice.

Chapter seven

It took longer than I expected for my return to Cromford House. After five weeks of interview sessions Rita found my replacement. He was called Gavin. He had short spikey hair and a passion for flowers that spread beyond the real kind because he liked to wear loud, floral shirts daily.

I worked a week with him, guiding him through the routines of the shop and quietly informing him on the likes and dislikes of Rita. He had a wicked sense of humour and was fun to work with. He also proved to have an originality with his flower arrangements, and it didn't take him long to prove his worth to Rita. I was a little disappointed that I was leaving as this was a relationship that I would have liked to see, well ... blossoming.

I gave my landlord notice on my flat and boxed up my belongings. By early April I was once more on the train back to Yorkshire. I arrived in Skipton very much as I had arrived back in Swansea two months previously: cold, tired, and hungry.

I had telephoned Lillian the day before to let her know what time I was expected at the train station. She had insisted that someone should be there to greet me and bring me home. It felt good that the house was being referred to as my home.

Once more I lugged my suitcase along the platform, until I saw Simon scanning the passengers looking for me. He was so tall and his red hair so vibrant that I could hardly have missed him.

I shouted across but an announcement drowned out my voice.

"Simon – over here," I shouted again.

He turned around and his face broke into a smile when he saw me. I felt a twinge of excitement as he strode towards me like a powerful Viking warrior on a conquest.

"Had a good trip?" He asked.

"Yes, but I seem to have hit the rush." I shouted above the noise of a diesel train powering up its engine on the platform behind me. "Let's get out of here!"

I followed him through the station. He had taken my suitcase and carried it with ease towards his Land Rover.

"Oh," I said in surprise as I saw Miranda sitting in the front passenger seat. "Hello Miranda, I hadn't expected to see you here."

"No, well, I had some things to deal with in town, and it seemed sensible to come with Simon." She spoke very casually in her smooth silky tones, not bothering to look at me but keeping her eyes firmly fixed on the windscreen.

I was disappointed that she had chosen to come. I had looked forward to a relaxed drive to the house.

The conversation back to Cromford House was stilted and uncomfortable, as was my position in the Land Rover. Miranda had said it would be too much of squeeze to sit in the front middle seat and suggested that I sat in the back. This meant that I was sat on one of the side benches. As there were no seat belts I slid about and had to cling to the body work when we went round a corner. I felt every bump and pothole and in addition, my view from the window was impaired.

Simon did his best to lighten the mood and tension between Miranda and myself, but his attempts at humour were poorly received by Miranda. I felt irritated by her attitude and embarrassed for Simon.

I knew very little about Simon except that he was our gamekeeper; and what I knew about game keeping I could have written on a postage stamp. He lived in a small annex of the house, ate his meals with the family and appeared to be on call twenty- four hours a day. If he had any social life, I had scarcely seen it during my first stay.

I had mixed feelings about seeing Simon on such an informal daily basis. He had a natural charm which could be described as chivalrous. This, coupled with his handsome features made him a very attractive man. I had already realised this at our first meeting and again today at the station watching the glances of several female passers-by. Yet oddly enough I did not feel attracted to him. Perhaps this was because he was somewhat older than myself as I guessed that he was in his early forties, but I did not feel this was quite the reason. No, there was something else about Simon, a ruthlessness, a kind of remote detachment that belied his good humour and charming smile that unnerved me.

As we approached the house my excitement grew. Even Miranda's presence didn't dampen my spirits. As the house came into view, albeit from a tiny side window, I felt a tremendous surge of joy and for the very first time I felt that I was indeed coming home.

It was still quite light as the days were noticeably lengthening and the clocks had moved forward. The garden was greener than when I had last seen it as many things had started to stir from their long winter's slumber.

We pulled into the courtyard and were greeted by the dogs barking excitedly as they came out to greet us. One gruff word from Simon and they stopped in their tracks, frozen to the spot, just their tails wagging furiously. Poor Charlie boy was so excited that he stood whimpering and whining, shaking uncontrollably, struggling to hold his excitement, but too afraid to risk Simon's displeasure. Simon took my case out of the back of the Land Rover and then helped me out before striding over to the dogs and stroking them both, talking to them in a quiet voice.

Lilian came out of the house and put her arms around me and gently kissed my cheek.

"Emily. It's so good to have you back again. How was your trip?"

"Horrendous!" I laughed.

"Was that the train or Simon's driving?" she mischievously asked grinning at Simon.

"We weren't sure if you would be delayed, so Janice has made a casserole for dinner."

"That's sound lovely," I said, "but what I really want is a nice cup of tea."

The casserole was delicious and the lemon meringue pie that followed was doubly so, and I had second helpings of both, travelling had made me rather hungry.

After dinner Miranda excused herself, claiming that she had paperwork to attend to. Lillian and I decided that we would leave Simon and Raymond to their brandy.

They were having a heated conversation over which 4x4 vehicle was the best-off road motor and never even noticed Lillian and I slip away.

I followed Lillian into the front sitting room, both of us choosing to sit by the fire as it was quite a chilly evening.

"I've been busy!" Lillian said in an excited manner as soon as we sat down.

"Busy?"

She nodded. "With detective work!"

I was intrigued.

"You recall Peter saying that my mother wanted to put things right and that her brother had been treated very unfairly by her father? Well, I decided to find out exactly what she meant. Peter was unable to help me as my mother had told him only very sketchy details, but he suggested that I might start trying to find my grandfather's will. He believed there was some sort of connection. So, I went in search of it."

"What, the will?"

She nodded hardly able to contain herself. "Yes, I did a lot of digging and with Peter's help I discovered two wills. The second, the most recently dated was of course the one that was used on his death, but we were lucky and discovered that the first will was still with another firm of solicitors and it was very different from the first."

"But lots of people change their wills Lillian for lots of reasons, it doesn't mean that much."

"That's exactly what Peter said. However, I am not convinced. Here take a look at it."

"You, have it?"

"Yes, I have both copies."

She got up and went to a little desk in the corner of the room, opened a drawer and slid out a manila-coloured envelope. "They're here," she said, her eyes sparkling.

She sat down and passed some old looking pieces of paper to me.

"That's the first will. It's worded very much the same as mum's and Edward Cromford is the named heir. In fact, he inherits everything. Mum has a good dowry but that's about it."

"Now, take a look at this." She passed me the other document that was very similar in appearance to the first. "That's the second will, look at the date at the top."

She pointed to the top right-hand corner of the will; it was five years after the first.

"Now," she continued. "Look at the third paragraph and read it aloud." I scanned down to the third paragraph, cleared my throat, and read aloud: "To my only child Roberta." I stopped and looked up. "You think that he thought that Edward had died?"

"Yes, that's what I thought – at first. But Emily if a child dies, you will of course change your will in favour of the surviving child but not erase them from your family history, and that is exactly what has happened here. Edward and his father may have had a massive disagreement over something which would give a plausible reason of course, but why would this have such a profound effect on my mother?

"So, I went to the city libraries to find something – anything, that related to the year that the new will was made."

"And did you find something?"

"Oh, yes. Prior to the new will been drawn up two local girls went missing."

I stared at her open mouthed, then swallowed hard. "Missing?"

"Yes." She leant towards me and whispered, "and one of them worked here, in Cromford House as a maid."

Lillian licked her lips and looked over her shoulder (who, or what she thought might be stood behind her and listening I had no idea).

She came even closer to me and said in a hushed tone that I had to strain to hear. "The girl was called Evelyn Slater. She was seventeen and had worked here for about a year. The other girl was Sarah Hardaker. She was nineteen and her body was found in the river two days after Evelyn's disappearance."

"Drowned?" I whispered back.

"Well," Lillian said leaning back in her chair and her normal voice returning.

"That was believed at first. It's a dangerous stretch of river here. A heavy downpour especially further up in the dale after a long dry spell can cause the river to rise two or three feet in minutes. It must go through a narrow channel when it reaches here you see, and it comes down in such a torrent it's all too easy to lose your footing on rocks that have become wet and slippery. The force of the water just sucks you under. Many people have lost their lives for centuries to that stretch. The old, ruined priory was, by all accounts, built in memory of one of the poor souls who drowned there.

It was thought that the girl had lost her footing and got swept away. That's what was reported in the papers."

She handed me some photocopied newspaper clippings. I didn't look at them. My eyes were firmly fixed on Lillian's as she continued.

"The coroner's report that came out a few weeks later said that she was dead before she went in the river. She had been strangled. It was also discovered that she was three months pregnant.

I gulped. "You mean she was ..."

"Murdered!" Lillian finished the sentence for me adding grimly, "There was a manhunt and who do you think the prime suspect was?"

"You don't mean ... you can't mean."

"I do: Edward Cromford disappeared the day before the girl's body was found and so did our little maid, but they never found her body, only some blood-stained clothing."

I felt physically sick. I had gone cold and was shaking. My grandfather a cold-blooded killer. I couldn't, just couldn't think about it. I got up and walked over to the fire, holding my hands out to the comforting flickering flames to warm myself although the chill I now felt I knew no fire could warm.

I turned from the fire and looked steadily at Lillian. I had to know, had to ask her. "Lillian", I said in a hoarse voice, "do you think he did it?"

She sat quietly for a moment or two, the ticking of the clock punctuating the stillness around us.

"I don't want to believe it, but the evidence is quite damning. It explains why he was shut out of the family. The new will and why my mother never mentioned him. Maybe she even hoped that he was dead. He would have been hanged had he been caught. When his father died Edward would have been no position to contest it. A wanted man could hardly turn up and claim his inheritance."

"No: of course not," I said slowly trying to understand the complexity of it all. "He would have been arrested the moment he announced himself. But Lillian, it's all so ... Horrible!"

"I know."

How old would Roberta have been when this happened?" I asked.

"Let me see." Lillian did some mental calculations, "thirteen or fourteen I think."

"It must have been very traumatic for her, having a brother do such a terrible thing. I wonder if they had been close?"

"Yes," Lillian agreed. "It must have affected her very deeply, and especially like you say if they had been close. I suspect that is why she never talked about him, removed all photos and all reference to him. I suppose it was like some type of therapy for her."

We both fell silent again, watching the flames in the fire wave about in their hypnotic dance, when a sudden thought struck me.

"Lillian, if this is true, why would your mother, after a lifetime of denying her brothers existence suddenly bring him back to life as it were. She certainly had no need to do so."

She thought for a moment before saying with a broad smile, "I think I need to do some more investigating."

I nodded. "Perhaps we both do."

I let out an involuntary yawn.

"I've kept you up too long," She apologised." I think it's time you went to bed, you have had a long and tiring day."

She took the paper clippings and the wills and slid them carefully back in the envelope before placing them in the desk drawer. She turned the key to the drawer and thoughtfully placed it in a small trinket pot on the mantel shelf.

"I think for the moment that we should we keep this to ourselves," she said.

"Yes, I agree, until we know more, I think that it would be for the best. Good night, Lillian."

"Good night." she smiled back.

As I made my way upstairs to bed the revelation about my grandfather went around in my head. Could he really have killed those girls? I felt sickened by the thought.

That night I dreamt that I was running along a riverbank, someone was behind me. I could hear their footsteps on the cold damp earth. I sensed an arm reach out towards me, a heavy breathing in my ear. I frantically tried to escape a man's tight grasp. I strained to see his face, but it was hidden in dark impenetrable shadows that refused to form into recognisable features. Then I was falling, falling into the icy waters of a river, my screams ripped away by its fury and all I could hear was the echoes of a man's laughter.

Chapter eight

I soon settled into life at Cromford House, which was lived at a much slower pace than in the city, and very soon I began to enjoy it.

Much of my time was spent in the garden; this was partly because I wanted to keep out of Miranda's way and, also because I needed to occupy myself. Roberta had often spent time in the garden too, helping with some of the tasks when her health permitted and so my presence was welcomed, unlike my presence in the house which was resented my Miranda.

I found that arranging plants in the ground was very similar to building a floral display and very soon I became engrossed in my new hobby. Although I had a vast knowledge of flowers and how to care for them when cut, I found that I was sadly lacking in their cultural needs. Robin however proved to be a willing teacher and would listen with interest to my ideas for bedding schemes. I was always delighted when a particular idea would work and disappointed when they would not. It was on these occasions that Robin would tactfully suggest a similar plant or flower that was more suited to the location I had in mind. His gardening knowledge never failed to amaze me, and I spent a lot of my time in his company: weeding, pricking out seedlings and general tidying around, and I found myself developing a strong attraction for him.

My evenings were spent shut away in the library, reading Roberta's old gardening books so that I could gain some knowledge of my own, and to find some new inspiration for the garden.

The library was one of my favourite rooms in the house. It was a small quiet room, and I became to regard it as my secret place, as a place of sanctuary and solitude where I could retreat from the rest of the household as no one else seemed to use it. I spent many happy hours in there curled up in one of the cosy chairs, listening to the logs quietly crackle in the fireplace with my head in a book and duchess snoozing at my feet.

My mother came to stay for a few days over the Easter holidays. The weather was unusually mild and dry. It was good to see her, although it was only a couple of weeks previously that I had left her in Swansea, but my life had changed so dramatically that it felt like a lifetime ago. She was impressed with the house and gardens, and for the first time in our lives, we sat down and talked openly about my father. We laughed and cried and felt all the better for it.

My mother was also a big hit with Lillian, and she even seemed to manage to penetrate the icy exterior of Miranda, who appeared to be much more tolerant towards my mother than me. If my mother noticed the tension between Miranda and myself, she never mentioned it. Neither Lillian nor I told her of the disturbing circumstances that surrounded Edward Cromford.

The day my mother left for home I stood on the steps of the house in the warm spring sunshine, a lump developing in my throat as I said my goodbyes. "You'll come back in the summer?" I asked noticing the note of hope in my voice.

"Just try and stop me." she said kissing me and wiping a stray tear that had started to trickle down my cheek.

I stood waving to her as the taxi finally disappeared round the last bend in the drive and she was gone.

I was quite saddened by mother's leaving and not wanting to pass my gloom on I decided that I would go for a walk down by the river where I could be alone.

I asked Janice if she would be kind enough to make me a packed lunch. I was of course quite capable of making my own lunch, but I had soon learnt that Janice was like a rottweiler on duty in her kitchen. Woe betide anyone who wandered in and started to assemble food on her watch and without authorisation. I pulled on a pair of sturdy boots and packed my sandwiches and tea in a rucksack, together with a waterproof coat and an ordnance survey map, just in case on both accounts.

Duchess came with me. Since my arrival at Cromford House she had become my shadow and I found that I enjoyed her gentle company. The other dogs in the house were working dogs, spending most of their time with Raymond or Simon. Duchess had once been a working dog, but a hip injury had left her slightly lame. Unable to keep up with the other dogs as they bounded through the heather, she became a hindrance. However, she had a lovely temperament and was very obedient, so she retired from her working life and was now pampered and a little overweight. Simon was pleased that I had taken to Duchess, or rather that she had taken to me and said that the gentle exercise she would get following me about would do her good.

So, duchess and I set off past the last daffodils of the season, their heads bobbing gently in the breeze.

Once I had reached the last terrace I headed straight to the bottom of the garden down towards the orchard, past the herbaceous borders. Here, row upon row of tulips were lined up, some of them were still tightly wrapped in their green jackets, but some had started to unfurl and display themselves with abandon in a glorious show of colour. When I reached the orchard, I stopped for a moment or two to admire its beauty: delicate pink and white blossom covered the fruit trees and was silhouetted against a clear blue sky looking like a delicate lace bridal gown.

At the end of the orchard the apple trees began to mingle with trees of oak and ash. The woodland was still quite bright as the sun was able to filter through the bare branches of the trees. In the summer months this would be a lovely cool retreat from the heat of the sun.

The floor of the wood was covered with hundreds of tiny white flowers of lesser stitchwort and milky wood anemones, their petals smudged with a faint blushing pink. I stopped to look at them. stooping down to admire the pretty delicate blossom.

The place was alive with birdsong. I tried to identify them. Great tit, wren, thrush, robin or was that a chaffinch? I made a mental note that next time I came here I would bring a bird book with me.

I followed the path deeper into the wood. I could hear the river and continued further into the trees with Duchess a little behind me until the river came into sight.

The path drew level with the water. It was a deep, rich shade of amber and was very wide and so clear that I could see the shingle on the riverbed. It flowed slow and even, except for a central channel where the water was turbulent. Here the water ran faster and darker – a deep coppery brown and the bottom disappeared from view.

There was a curious clicking noise. I looked around to see where it was coming from. A border collie popped its head up from the overhang of the riverbank and sitting next to the dog was a fisherman. He was so well concealed that I had not previously noticed him. The clicking sound was the reel of his rod as he wound in the line and then swiftly cast out again. He sat very still, his eyes fixed on the orange tip of the float as it was swept along in the central channel of the fast-moving water.

The dog gave out a low growl, causing the man to break his concentration and turn around to see what his dog had seen.

He was an older man, with white hair that stuck out in tufts around the edges of his tweed cap. He paled when he saw me, the colour visibly draining from his face, Intensifying the blue of his eyes. At the sudden shock of my appearance, he dropped his fishing rod with a clump and a clatter.

"I'm sorry," I said. "I didn't mean to startle you."

The sound of my voice seemed to break the spell that my appearance had cast over him and he regained his composure.

"Easy, Bess," he mumbled to the dog and reached out and patted her softly on the neck. Then he retrieved the fishing rod and began to wined in the line.

"Thought you were the water bailiff!" he chuckled.

"Oh, I see, I am sorry," I said again.

"No matter, no harm done," he said looking at the rod. He cast out once more and then reached into his pocket and pulled out a pipe. He stuffed a bit of tobacco in the end of it, struck a match and put it to the tobacco and methodically began to puff on the pipe. His dog saw Duchess as she finally caught up with me and bounded over to her, the two dogs obviously having met before.

He took the pipe from his mouth and waved it in the general direction of the house. "You're the new Cromford girl." It was a statement not a question.

I inwardly groaned. Did everyone know my business?

"Yes – how do you know?"

"The lab." Once more he pointed with his pipe, this time towards Duchess. He whistled to his dog who came obediently to sit by his side.

"I thought this was private land?" I said wrinkling my nose up at the smell of the tobacco smoke drifting in the air, and at the same time hoping that I didn't sound too pompous.

"It is." he said with a wry smile and not a hint of embarrassment.

"Oh," was all I could reply to his calm answer.

"Going for a walk?" he asked quite unconcerned that he was trespassing, and poaching no doubt too given his reaction to the possibility that I was the water bailiff.

I decided that it was probably best to overlook his whereabouts as I really had no idea if he had permission to be here or not. "Yes, I thought I would follow the river and stop somewhere for lunch. It's such a lovely day."

"I'll let you get off then." He took another thoughtful puff on his pipe and then turned once more to study the river; I had the strangest feeling that I was being dismissed.

"Mind how you go." He called after me, the smoke from his pipe encircling him. "The river gets dangerous further down and the rocks can be slippery."

I waved my hand in thanks and set off downstream, Duchess slowly following me.

It was pleasant walking along the river. I loved the sound of the bird song and the gurgling water as it swirled past. Duchess began to lag further and further behind as we started to climb, and I realised that her hip was starting to bother her as we began to follow the path away from the river on a steep incline.

I waited patiently for her to catch up and stroked her smooth head when she drew level with me. "Just a little further," I said soothingly to her.

I wanted to have lunch where the river narrowed and flowed into a rocky channel. It was the part of the river that I had heard about, and that the fisherman had warned me of. I was aware of the dangers and had no intention of straying too close. I slowed my pace so Duchess could keep up with me and very soon we were looking down on the water of the river. I could see that already it had started to gather speed as it began to flow into a deeply carved channel of rock. The tone of the water had also changed; instead of the melodious carefree gurgle it had gathered rhythm and was now gushing and splashing in excitement and little white crests of water spun on the top.

As the path once more began to drop down to the river the path changed from compacted earth to rock and the noise of the river increased, as the water now began to surge through an and ever narrowing channel. As we cleared the trees and once more became level with the river, we were walking on bare rock that was covered with a thin layer of green moss. Today it was quite dry, but if wet I could see how treacherous it could be. There were warning signs dotted about on several trees and two life rings strapped to sturdy metal posts: one on either side of the river. We had come to a stretch of the river where it turned into a violent monster. Thick creamy white foam spun about on the surface of the water, and it had turned so dark that it almost looked black.

Thousands of gallons of water was being churned and forced through a narrow channel in the rock that the foolhardy could jump or stride over. Locally, this stretch of the river was called the striddings for that very reason and had earned its deadly reputation from those fools that had tried and then paid the ultimate price by losing their footing on the surrounding rocks and fallen prey to the river, only to be sucked under and battered to death by the current as it smashed their soft bodies into unforgiving rocks and then swept them on downstream.

Their mutilated remains would be found, sometimes days later, tossed aside by the power of the water.

I sat down on a dry rock well away from the water's edge, gently clipping Duchess to her lead in case she wandered off and became another victim of the river.

It was such a beautiful spot. The sun filtered through the branches of the trees whose young and tender leaves were a tiny and transparent fresh green. The ground was littered with spent beech nuts, and I watched a grey squirrel search among them hoping to find an unopened case or two.

My mind began to drift to my grandfather, and I wondered if he used to come and sit by the river like this. On the opposite side of the bank a pair of grey wagtails began to flit about, and I realised how alone I was. There was no sound other than that of the river, its gushing fury filling the air, while the spray that it made cast miniature rainbows above the rock in the spring sunshine.

I remembered what Lillian had said about the girl who had been murdered and how her broken body had been found in the river only a day or two after my grandfather had disappeared.

Did he follow her here, or perhaps arrange to meet her and then murder her? The noise of the river drowning out her screams for help. Could he have really been capable of such a thing? I shuddered as a feeling of fear, revulsion, and my own vulnerability crept over me.

Duchess laid her warm head in my lap sensing my shift in mood, reminding me that I was not alone, and I had her protection.

I looked down into her eyes and fondled one of her soft velvet ears. "Quite right too," I whispered. "Now let's see what we have dinner?"

With that she lifted her head and began to wag her tail in anticipation, my sombre mood lifting.

Chapter nine

The days grew longer and warmer, while the garden grew greener. As the end of May came into sight, I became eager to plant out the bedding and see my design schemes in the ground. Robin told me that I would need to be patient and wait until the very end of May until all danger of frost would be over, so I waited; but not so patiently.

All my attention now was focused on the garden. What had started out as merely a way to pass the time had turned into an all-consuming hobby and, much to my dismay I found that it gobbled money at an alarming rate.

After doing some calculations in the library one wet and dreary afternoon I concluded that by the end of the year all my savings would be gone and that my income would barely cover my outgoings. I had committed to finish the pond system and had been told by Peter that I would have to pay for this myself as the trust fund would not be able to be used for the project.

I began to wonder if I could run the garden as a business. Opening more days to the public, hiring it out for special events such as birthdays, weddings, and social gatherings, perhaps even organising events of my own. The more I thought about it the more plausible it became. A large part of the stable block was unused, I could turn it into tea rooms with a lovely outdoor seating area and make a small garden centre area. Perhaps I could include a flower shop which would be an added advantage for special occasion parties and may be a gallery for my pictures and ask other local artists if they would like to display their work and have an opportunity to sell it too. Perhaps we could also do some catering for events? My imagination began to run away with itself, and I became excited by the notion. Money was going to be the stumbling point, but the trust fund would pay in part for the refurbishment of the stable block as this would fall under building maintenance but the rest I would have to borrow.

The first person I told was Robin. I had grown to trust him and valued his opinions, besides I felt that the garden belonged to him as well as myself as he put so much into his work and that any plans regarding its future should involve him and, of course Tom.

Robin listened to my plans with interest, Tom was less enthusiastic: he just didn't like the idea of lots of people.

However, with a little gentle persuasion from Robin and my assurance that the potting shed and the furthest greenhouse would not have public access and that he would not have to mix – or speak to anyone if he didn't wish to – then he came round a little.

I took the opportunity to speak to Lillian and Raymond one evening over dinner while Miranda was otherwise engaged. I knew she would look at my idea with scorn and only dampen my enthusiasm.

"I have been thinking," I began hesitantly, "that I might open the gardens to the public more days of the week and," I faltered, "hire them out for weddings and special occasions."

I regarded them both closely. Raymond continued eating his dinner piercing a carrot forcefully and Lillian took a sip of wine and looked across at Raymond.

"I think that would be a lovely idea, don't you Raymond?" she said.

"Yes, I suppose so," he replied in a rather disinterested manner.

"I also thought that maybe that I could convert the old stable block into a tearoom and incorporate a flower shop, I could also supply space for local artists to show their work. I thought that there would be space by the greenhouses to have a small garden centre area."

Raymond stopped eating and put down his knife and fork. "You're planning quite a business adventure there Emily. Have you thought about cost and funding?"

"Well," I began. "I haven't got any quotes for the building work, but I thought that I would be allowed to use some of the trust fund money for the conversion of the stable block. As for the rest I thought that I could go to the bank and apply for a business loan."

"I see," Raymond said reaching for his wine glass. "Put together a business plan, with projected costs and profits and let me look at it. If I think it's practical then I'll lend you the money, don't really like banks, don't trust them. They rob you blind with fees. It will be a proper loan though. Peter would see to all the legal details."

I was stunned, I didn't know what to say except "thank you."

He waved his fork about, a piece of beef dripping gravy back onto his plate. "Don't need to thank me. I'm only lending out the money you're the one with all the hard work ahead of you."

Lillian looked at her husband and then said, "the gardens could be opened up for events now though?"

Raymond shrugged. "We'd need permission from the council, probably some sort of licence: they will charge a bit for that, but we have the facilities. I don't really see much of a problem, it's not that much different from the shooting parties. I'll check to see if our insurance covers us. I expect they will want a payment for that too. There are far too many greedy buggers who do nothing but want payment for all that red tape nonsense."

Lillian beamed at him and then said to me, "I don't want to interfere, but my friend runs the amateur dramatics society, and she has been itching to hold an outdoor venue ever since she went to one herself. I think the gardens would be the perfect setting and would kick start off your little venture."

"Oh, Lillian that would be lovely, what production did she have in mind?"

"A Midsummer Night's Dream, and I think that if we pulled out all the stops, we could actually get to hold it on midsummer's day."

"How perfect."

On the very last day of May I was sitting in the dining room munching on my third piece of toast having already demolished two boiled eggs. Working outside in the garden had given me an extraordinary appetite and I now had the added excitement of running it as a business. I was busily jotting down a list of things that I needed to do for the event that was now only a month away when Simon walked in.

"Good morning," he said.

I looked up startled. It was not customary for Simon to join us for breakfast, he was usually up at a very early hour, and it was the norm for him to have his morning break sat at the kitchen table with Janice fussing over him.

"Emily, would you like to come up onto the moor today?"

Ever since my arrival at Cromford House the moor had enchanted me, but as yet I had not explored it.

"I'd love too, but I'm not sure I have the time, there is so much to do here ..."

"A few hours won't hurt your plans. It's a perfect day of blue skies and no rain or wind in the forecast."

I was torn. I did indeed have a mountain of things to do. Lillian had spoken to her friend, and it had been arranged that our first event was to be an outdoor performance of a *Midsummer Night's Dream*. We all thought that the garden would create a magical setting and it was planned to take place on midsummer evening. There was to be champagne and strawberries in the interval and then a moonlight tour of the garden after the performance. We would use small handheld lanterns and I had planned to place fairies around the garden creating beautiful dells and magical places for pixies and sprites to hide, all in keeping with Shakespeare's tale. The event had been advertised in the local press and radio and was titled: An enchanted evening. To my delight tickets were selling rapidly. In addition to all this planning I was also aiding with the planting of the bedding schemes that were due to start that morning,

"It a beautiful day!" Simon said again, "shame to miss the opportunity."

Simon was right. It was a beautiful day, and a few hours wouldn't really make that much of a difference, and it would be nice to have a brief break. "Ok, you have twisted my arm then." I agreed.

He smiled and pulled out a chair then poured himself a coffee.

Miranda who had silently been sat at the head of the table lowered the paper she was reading. She gazed over the edge of it with just her beautiful blue eyes showing. She looked like an exotic Eastern princess.

"It has been such a long time since I have been out on the moor. Would you mind if I tagged along?" she said watching Simon "I feel the fresh air would do me good."

I sat back in my chair surprised at her request. Annoyed, but not surprised that she had asked Simon and not me if she could join us. Miranda had never expressed any interest in the moor other than its financial value, but I knew so little about her. She was an enigma to me: beautiful, serene, and unfathomable.

Simon glanced at her, with what I thought was irritation. If she noticed, then she pretended not to, and I had an odd feeling of alarm that Simon might have wanted to be alone with me.

He shrugged, "Yes, if you like," he said to her.

An hour later we were assembled on the top terrace, each of us carrying a rucksack that had been so crammed full of food by Janice that they could have been mistaken for a fortnight's survival pack in the wilderness. It would have been pointless for us to refuse her offerings of food, so we quietly accepted and said our thanks staggering away under the weight of our bags.

Duchess sat watching me with wistful brown eyes. She was to stay behind as she would need to be on her leash because of the young chicks and this would have made walking with her slow progress.

We set off down the drive towards the main gate. In the background I could hear Duchess mournfully howling. "Keep on walking," Simon told me. "And don't look back. She'll stop soon enough."

I felt mean leaving her and wished that I hadn't agreed to come. We walked down the drive in a little procession, our boots softly clumping along the grey tarmac in a smooth rhythm while the howls became a faint melancholy sound in the distance.

A car swung into the gates at the bottom of the drive, and I recognised it to be that of Robin's. He drew to a halt at the side of us and wound down the car window.

He nodded towards Miranda and Simon, "Good morning, Miss Maxwell, Simon." Then he turned to me, "going out for a walk?"

I said "yes," and he smiled.

"I don't know, all these weeks of nagging about getting the plants in and on the first day that we are going to start you go gallivanting off!"

"Do you mind?" I was suddenly worried that he would be.

He grinned, "No of course not. You go off and enjoy yourself and don't think about me on my hands and knees trying to fathom out your planting schemes."

"I'll see you later this afternoon then," and laughed.

"Probably." Then he turned to Simon. "Where are you going then?"

"God's seat," Simon replied.

Robin frowned. God's seat was an outcrop of giant-sized boulders that perched on top of the moor. I had heard of walkers losing their way in thick fog and plummeting to their death over the edge. Today however it was clear and bright, and I could see no cause for concern for our destination. Nevertheless, a troubled look crossed Robin's face. "Be careful up there, Emily. Keep away from the edge."

"I will," I promised.

Satisfied with my reply, but still concerned he said. "Well, some of us have work to do," and drove off waving.

"Really," said Miranda after he had gone. "You shouldn't let him speak to you like that, Emily."

"Like what?" I enquired. I was still smiling after him and wishing that he was taking me out today instead of Simon.

"Like he's in charge, you're the one who pays his wages. You can do whatever you choose to do, you don't need his permission!"

I didn't want to spoil the day by arguing with her but felt angry at her comment. I had been apprehensive about her coming on a walk with us and I had no intention of having to endure her frosty silence for the rest of the day. I noticed that Simon had an amused look on his face. One of his eyebrows was raised at what I thought was disbelief at Miranda's sometimes priggish high handedness. Unable to stop myself I sharply said, "I really don't think that it is any your business."

She pursed her lips, and I thought how funny she looked in her fluorescent jacket and clumpy boots, with an oversized rucksack strapped to her back and her lady of the manner attitude. Her eyes narrowed as she was about to say something, but Simon interrupted her, and said in a gruff voice, "for goodness sakes Miranda, let it go. Emily is right. It really is none of your business."

I thought for a moment that this would signify trouble, but Miranda turned abruptly away so that I could not see her face and her fists clenched tightly into little white balls but remained silent.

It was a good day for a walk. It had rained during the night, but the sky had cleared and now it was deep blue, punctuated with soft billowing clouds of purest white. The sun reflected from the crest of each cloud and gave them a brilliant luminescent glow. The earth smelt sweet, and damp and the smell of grass permeated the air on a gentle breeze as we crossed a meadow.

Simon had a wonderful knowledge of the wildlife. He was able to name every bird either by sight or sound, and much to my surprise he was able to name the many wildflowers. He also knew much about the land and of its history.

Simon talked steadily about the area, of past and present farming, a little about the pheasant and grouse shoot and how he managed the game. I found his information fascinating.

There was a glint in his eyes when he spoke, a glint that I had not previously seen, and I learnt much about Simon that day. He was not only enthusiastic about the land but the people and creatures that inhabited it, and indeed the people who had once lived there. He pointed out the old ruins of a medieval village where all the inhabitants had died of the plague, and an old Saxon settlement.

There was no trace of sentiment with Simon. He just related the facts. He would have been as capable as watching a fox, admiring its slim streamline body, the grace of her movements and the glory of her beautiful fur and then just as easily shoot it dead. There would be no malicious intent or cruelty involved in his actions just a simple equation: the fox or the game, there was no room for remorse or regret, the end justified the means.

The track up to the moor was steep. Some of it was open, with the odd scruffy sheep and her much cleaner and tidier looking lambs grazing on the already cropped grass. We passed a pair of lambs snoozing under a hawthorn tree, its branches were heavy and bent with the weight of the blossom it bore and the air sweet with its scent. The lambs started when they saw us and ran loudly bleating towards their mother who was a little further up the track. With her offspring safely hidden behind her she glared at us and let out a disdainful bleat. Then she set off scornfully down the track with her two lambs obediently following.

As the track wound round, we entered a conifer plantation, how different the atmosphere was here, so cool and still. The sun had been banished and the ground was covered in a dense mat of rust coloured pine needles and black dead twigs and branches. There was strange hush about the place and for some odd reason we began to whisper.

I was glad once more when we emerged into the bright sunshine, and I realised to my delight that we had climbed a great deal. Looking back, I could see Cromford House, the stone terraces and the driveway winding its way towards the house.

"The moor is just over there," said Simon, pointing to a drystone wall that cut the track in two and then ran off down the hill until it was obscured by trees. In the opposite direction up the hill it was swallowed by fresh green bracken and heather.

We struggled through the stile owing to the size of our rucksacks, or to be more precise the size of our sandwich boxes and had to take them off to climb over and through the tiny gap.

The path was now little more than a peat track and weaved its way on through the shrubby heather. Suddenly a bird's head popped out of a thick clump of vegetation not far from me. She made a soft clucking sound in the back of her throat and watched me warily with bright, jet-like eyes.

"It's a grouse, see theirs her chicks," Simon whispered in my ear and pointed to what could only be described as mottled brown and dull yellow fluffy pom-poms with stick-like legs that bobbed up and down on top of the heather. They were adorable and I wanted to scoop them up into my hands and feel their thistle down softness. I knew of course that would be impossible and even if it were, Simon would most certainly disapprove.

We walked for about another half hour, surrounded by the gentle clucking of grouse, the high-pitched calls of the lapwings and the eerie lonely cry of curlews until we reached the huge outcrop of rock that was referred to locally as God's Seat.

Miranda, her mood having lifted, said, "My grandmother used to bring me here as a child."

I don't think that I'd ever seen Miranda looking as beautiful as she did at that moment, her hair was blowing in the breeze and her cheeks were flushed a soft pink with the exertion of the climb. She smiled at me, a genuine smile. Her eyes were wide and sparkling with excitement, and for the briefest of moments I saw the vibrant woman behind the thick impenetrable armour that she normally wore. With each step we took the ridge began to take shape, looming higher and higher and steeper and steeper into the sky. Great stones the size of houses lay about stacked on top of each other and reached ever up wards towards heaven.

We approached from the side, and I could see the sheer drop that the stones formed as they clung to the edge of the hillside.

"The rocks are made of hard grit," said Miranda. "Bobby – that's what I called my grandmother – said they were left here in the last ice age, and that they were dragged by the glaciers and deposited as they started to melt. The melted water and thousands of years of rain has eroded the natural limestone leaving this unlikely cliff face. The glaciers formed the dales too, by gouging their way across the county. What you see today is what they left in their wake."

I smiled at her and once again she smiled at me. It was a smile like her mother's, warm, friendly, and open. Perhaps I thought, like the glaciers Miranda was beginning to thaw and maybe, just maybe a new landscape could be forged between us.

We scrambled our way along the last of the rocks, they had a rough sandy texture that grazed my hands.

Once on the summit rock I gazed about. This was truly a seat for a god. You could see for miles and miles. Dale upon dale swelled up in the distance like waves on a still and silent sea of misty green and hazy grey.

I shivered; there was a cold, strong breeze. I pulled on my jacket and woolly hat, and we took shelter behind one of the rocks to eat our mammoth-sized lunch.

I had always been fond of Greek legends, and now I fancied myself looking down from Mount Olympus. It was a silly childhood fantasy I know, but I felt in this magical place that was so far from the world below, anything was possible. Perhaps, even that the barriers that lay between Miranda and me could be swept aside and we could start anew. A feeling of fresh hope and optimism swelled inside of me, and I felt liberated and excited.

I noticed that there was another path besides the one that we were on. It went at right angles to the path that we were following, in the opposite direction and crossed the moor in an undulating fashion, hiding sections of itself from view until it reached the great slabs of rock that we were sat on.

"Where does that path lead?" I enquired.

"It goes down into the next dale to a village there, the whole moorland belongs to the estate, but the path is a right of way," Miranda told me.

"You get a really clear view of Cromford House from over here," Simon called out to me.

I turned my back on the other path and went over to where Simon was stood leaving my rucksack on the ground with Miranda. Simon was stood quite close to the edge and as I have never had a good head for heights, I stopped a little way from him.

"Come on Emily," he laughed. "You will have to come a little closer than that." He held out his arm towards me. "Here, take my hand."

I shuffled a little closer to him not daring to take my eyes off the rock edge. I felt his hand firmly grip mine and pull me gently towards him. As I drew level with him, he pointed with his free hand. "There look, Cromford House. Doesn't it look amazing? And the gardens and the greenhouses too, you can see it all."

He was behind me now, having moved his body round so that I could get a better view. He spoke softly in my ear, and I began to feel myself relax as he pointed out various landmarks. I moved a little closer to the edge.

Who was that tiny figure on the middle terrace? I was about to ask who he thought it might be when I let out a scream. I felt myself lurch forward, the rock that had been under my feet was no longer there. I had the sensation of slipping, and somewhere from behind there was another high-pitched scream.

Then a vice-like grip on my waist as I was violently pulled back, the rock scraping my legs.

"Is she all, right?" asked someone in an unfamiliar voice.

I blinked at a man's concerned, wrinkled face, and then at Simon's ashen one.

"What ... happened?" My voice sounded dazed and unfamiliar.

"You slipped," Simon said grimly.

"You're lucky this chap grabbed you or else ..." he didn't need to finish his sentence. His expression said it all. A woman appeared over the man's shoulder.

"Is she all right Arthur?" she demanded in a shrill voice. "We had just come over the hill on the other path and we saw you tumble. It was horrible. We thought you were a goner for sure."

She took hold of my hands. Suddenly I had gone cold, so very, very cold and I began to tremble and shake.

"Arthur, where's the thermos. This lass needs a warm drink. She's in shock."

He handed her a bright blue and yellow flask and she poured some hot steaming liquid into the vivid blue cup. "You." She looked at Simon. "Help her over to that rock and get her to drink this," she said to Simon who mutely obeyed.

"I know it should be hot sweet tea, but we only have coffee, but Arthur likes a lot of sugar so I think it will do," she said.

Once I had sat down, I gratefully drank the hot milky liquid. It was very sweet and with each mouthful I began to feel a little better. When the woman was satisfied that I was all right she handed Arthur the empty thermos which he dutifully took and put away and put in his backpack.

"I am sorry, I seem to have drunk all your coffee," I said feebly to him.

"Never mind lass, you're okay and that's all that matters. Could have been a terrible tragedy," he said solemnly shaking his head.

"Yes," I nodded. "Thank you."

"It's not me that's needs thanking it's this lad here." He motioned to Simon. "If it weren't for him then, well ..."

The woman, who I presumed to be Arthur's bossy wife said, "Right, if you're sure you're okay we'll be on our way, won't we Arthur?"

"Righto dear, on our way then." He merrily replied and they set off together across the heather.

When they were out of sight, I mumbled my apologies to Miranda and Simon. I felt like a stupid fool, ashamed of my clumsiness. Neither of them spoke. Miranda's face was white, all the glowing freshness of only minutes ago had vanished and she looked drawn and tired. The sparkle in her beautiful blue eyes had disappeared and were now deadened, wide and staring with a look of horror.

Simon was silent, his face white and full of fear.

Chapter ten

It was the following day before I saw Robin. I was on my hands and knees by one of the flower beds planting out some small bush fuchsia. In a few short weeks they would be smothered in flowers of rich shades of red and purple.

"Where did you get to yesterday?" he asked as he strolled up beside me.

"I was tired," I mumbled keeping my eyes fixed on the dark, crumbly soil in front of me, as I recalled the events of yesterday.

Miranda, Simon, and I had walked home in silence. All the joviality of the outing was lost, overshadowed by my foolish clumsiness. I felt utterly miserable. Any hope of reconciliation with Miranda had been destroyed. She was despondent and withdrawn, her opinion of me now sinking deep into the depths of contempt.

Simon had suggested that it would be better if we were not to mention the incident, it would only cause alarm and upset to others if we were to do so. Miranda agreed with him, and I saw no reason to do otherwise.

On that long and silent walk back to Cromford House I began to doubt myself. Perhaps I should go back to Swansea, I didn't really belong here. I could go back to my old life, my friends, familiar surroundings with familiar faces: it was a comforting prospect. Yet deep down inside I knew that running away was not the answer. Edward Cromford had run from his responsibilities and had left nothing but destruction in his wake. I would not run away from mine. I would be handing them down to another generation like some disregarded toy.

I found myself going over and over the sequence of events: how had I slipped? Was I really so close to the edge? I wasn't sure. Simon was behind me. Miranda must have been very close because I remember her shrill screams and then I began to think that perhaps she had pushed me. The more I went over the event the more plausible it became. I shut out the thought. I was still upset. No matter how much she disliked me, I could not; would not think that she had done such a thing. I was trying to pin the blame on someone else, and not admit my own careless stupidity. And yet, there was something in the back of my mind, had I felt a push in the small of my back?

Robin knelt beside me and picked up a tray of deep pink Bizzie – Lizzie. "Are these going in too?" he asked.

I nodded.

"In a row?"

"No, I want them in a drift."

He gently eased the small plants out of their containers and laid them carefully on the soil spacing them apart, so they formed a sweeping pattern.

"Like this?"

"Yes."

He sighed, took a side long glance at me, and shrugged. He was aware that something was troubling me. I watched him for a few minutes as he made a hole in the earth and then eased the plant into it, smoothing the soil softly about it, like he was tucking it into bed with a tenderness that came naturally to him.

"What did you think of God's seat?" he suddenly asked.

The question took me by surprise. I took a sharp intake of breath, and my eyes widened in dismay. What should I say? I faltered, my mind racing, then said rather evasively. "Oh ... it was ... lovely."

"You don't sound too sure."

"Oh, no. it really was lovely." I said hastily in a voice that sounded false and far too bright.

I turned away from him, so he was unable to see my face.

He sat back on his haunches, and I became acutely aware of him watching me, his eyes penetrating deep, seeing things that I wanted to keep hidden.

I reached for another fuchsia and roughly turned it over in its pot, before brutally thumping the bottom and tugging it out.

"Careful," he softly warned. "They have fragile stems. You'll break it if you're too rough.

"I'm not being rough." I snapped back, shoving the plant in the hole that I had just dug, then forcibly pushing the soil around its base.

I was frustrated and angry with myself. Wishing now that I had not promised Miranda and Simon to keep quiet about yesterday's incident. But if I had been able to tell, would I also have said that I believed Miranda had pushed me. Would Robin think I was mad? I believed that I was mad for having such a notion.

I sat silently looking at the little fuchsia that I had just so brutally mutilated. One of its branches was hanging limply down and several of its leaves were crushed and bruised. Robin didn't deserve to be on the receiving end of my temper any more than the poor little plant.

"I'm sorry," I said in a deflated voice.

"Don't worry, it'll pick up," Robin said quietly as he deftly removed the broken branch and damaged leaves.

I turned to him. "I didn't mean the plant. I mean I am sorry I snapped at you."

Robin grinned, "I know." His eyes were twinkling at me. Then he looked at me quietly and said seriously. "You have been working hard Emily trying to get the business up and running. I know money's tight and ..." he hesitated, "I know that things between you and Miss Maxwell are well ... there is friction between you two."

"You know?" I could feel tears begin to prick my eyes.

"News travels fast round here!" He was of course referring to Janice our number one broadcasting station. "What you need is a break. Look, we will have most of the bedding in by the end of the week. Why don't you come out with me on Saturday? We could go out for the day and call in for something to eat on the way home."

I felt a twinge of excitement in my stomach. Was he asking me out on a date?

"I'd love too," I said.

Robin came to pick me up at ten on Saturday morning. We had arranged to visit some water gardens of a stately home called Feather Rails which was only an hour's drive away.

I was like a silly teenager trying to get dressed. My bed was covered in discarded outfits and now the floor was also covered. This was madness. I saw Robin every day, in just an old pair of jeans or shabby skirt worn with wellies and a bobbly jumper. In the end I settled for the first item that I had pulled out of my wardrobe. It was a sleeveless cotton dress that had always been a favourite of mine.

It had a tightly fitted bodice that swept into a knee length full skirt which had a bold printed border of pansies in varying shades of lilac and blue. They spread upwards towards the bodice of the dress slowly petering out so that just random tiny flowers were scattered on the top of the dress.

I picked up a light cardigan in a deep blue should it get cooler and made my way to the front steps of the house where I waited nervously for Robin.

I had previously shut Duchess in the kitchen with her breakfast so she was busily occupied and would not see me leave. I hoped that she would not make too much of a fuss when she realised that I was gone.

I had only been waiting for a minute or two when I saw his car coming towards the house and my stomach began fluttering with butterflies. "You look nice," he said as he got out of the car and walked round to open the passenger door for me. He was wearing his usual uniform of faded jeans and a t-shirt, although they were clean and pressed and looked new, his hair was loosely flopping into his face, and he smelt clean and fresh. I could smell a cedar wood aftershave in the air and his sunglasses made him look cool. My stomach did a little somersault.

I looked down at the dress I was wearing suddenly afraid that it was inappropriate.

"Am I overdressed?" I asked.

"No," he smiled, "I think you look perfect."

We spoke very little on the journey to Feather Rails. We often worked side by side in the garden without speaking very much, there was never any awkwardness in our silences, just a lovely feeling of togetherness.

We entered the grounds of the estate through a stone archway via a tree-lined avenue.

A herd of deer was roaming in the fields on each side of the roadway and the house was clearly visible at the end creating a grand vista. It was of a pale creamy coloured stone which seemed to lack substance. Intricate carvings and delicate little facets adorned the windows and doors of the house giving it a superficial look of femininity. I compared it to Cromford House: stone built, practical, a solid, unfussy type of house that had also stood the test of time.

I was surprised with the gardens at Feather Rails, although they complimented the house beautifully, they were so simple and elegant in style given the fuss and pomp of the house. I had expected frilly flowerbeds and fussy plantings, but the garden was simplistic in design using single plantings of one type of flower in the same colour, creating bold striking schemes. Each part of the garden effortlessly flowed into the next creating a soothing and tranquil space. The dominating feature of the garden was a river which ran through it.

Robin told me that house and the garden had been created in the seventeenth century by the architect owner, and that the river had been the starting point for the whole design of the garden. It had been forced to run into a series of pools, rills, and waterfalls before it finally ran into a large crescent shaped lake ending in a cascade over a weir where once more it was then able to flow freely down one of the prettiest tree-lined valleys that I had ever seen. At the very end of the garden a mile away from the house where it was then allowed to flow over a weir and continue its journey to the sea unhindered. It was so tranquil, just the sound of the running water and pools reflecting the green of the trees and the blue of the sky. At various points in the garden, we came across little follies and stone arbours and temples, a token of the architect's leanings.

We sat on a bench in one of the open fronted temples enjoying the coolness of the marble against our skin. It was a hot day. And it was a relief to be out of the sun's scorching heat. We looked out at an expanse of grass that had swathes of tiny white daises running through it. In the centre of the lawn and opposite us was a circular pond, and at its centre was a statue of a bare maiden. Water nymphs were gathered at her feet, two in her hair and she cradled one in her outstretched hands.

Sparkling Sunkissed water trickled over her fingers and onto her bare legs, before slipping back into the pond creating a beautiful scene and a tranquil melody.

"Mum, used to bring me and my sister here," Robin said. "It's the reason I wanted to become a gardener."

I turned to look at him smiling. We were sitting very close. "What did your family think about you wanting to be a gardener?"

"Dad wasn't too pleased, he wanted me to go on to engineering like himself. Thought that gardening was a sissy's job. He came round though once I got a job at the parks department, and he was dead proud when I got myself a place at the college and got my qualifications."

I felt Robin's hand reach for mine and a shiver of pleasure as his rough dry fingers encircled my hand. Struggling to ignore the thrilling sensation of his hand caressing mine I said, "And then you came to Cromford House."

"Yes, one of my tutors was a friend of Mrs Cromford's she was looking for another gardener and my tutor suggested me."

"I'm glad," I said.

He pushed a stray curl of hair away from my face and idly wound it round his finger. I gazed up into his eyes. They appeared to be a deep green reflecting the lush colour of the grass about us.

"So am I." He whispered bringing his face close to mine so that it became a blur. Then I knew what it was like to kiss those soft pink lips that I had so often dreamt about, and it was even more delicious and exciting than I had ever imagined.

We left the little temple hand in hand, wandering along the gravel path silent and content in the company of one another.

It was late afternoon before we left Feather Rails. The day had been gloriously hot, and the evening looked as though it would be too. We stopped at a little Italian restaurant for our meal and bought a bottle of wine to take home with us. By the time we pulled up at Robin's cottage on the outskirts of the village the sky was a rich vermillion red. Wispy ribbons of cloud high up reflected the last of the sun's rays turning them a deep blush pink as it slowly slid behind the hills.

Robin's cottage was in a row of eight other cottages. They were all stone built and had a small enclosed front garden with a straight flagged path that led to the front door.

I followed Robin along the path to his door when he stopped and waved to a man who was passing along the street.

"Evening Bill," Robin called out to him.

The man stopped by Robin's open gate and his dog wandered in to greet Robin.

"Evening," the man said and then turned to me, "Miss" with a slight nod of his head.

It was the same gentleman that I had encountered a month or two previously on the riverbank. He and Robin chatted about this and that and I kept noticing that the man's eyes kept drifting towards me as they were talking. There was something that made me feel uncomfortable under his gaze, and I became anxious to escape those prying eyes.

"So, this is the young lady that you have told me about?" he said to Robin now turning his attention fully on me.

Robin blushed a little. Winked at me and then said, "Yes. This is Miss Emily Cromford."

Bill smiled a secret smile. "Aye, well time I was getting on."

"Nice old bloke," Robin said once Bill was out of earshot. "Lives on his own a few doors down. Moved here about eighteen months ago after his wife died. I pop in now and then to do odd jobs and a bit of shopping."

"I've met him before," I said, "down on the river – fishing."

"Poaching, was he?" Robin laughed.

"I think so, I think he was on the private stretch."

Robin laughed. "Sounds about right. Bill told me that he lived in the village when he was a boy and would often go fishing down there. Think he got a thrill out of poaching. Looks like he still does."

I laughed and followed Robin through his front door, but my second encounter with Bill had left me as uneasy as my first.

Robin's home was small and compact, everything very neat and tidy. In the front room there was a comfortable looking armchair in a dark chenille type of fabric. It was well worn but clean and at right angles to it was a much newer looking small sofa in a deep beige colour. In the corner of the room was a portable TV, and an alcove with shelves that was piled with books and gardening magazines.

The daylight had almost faded now so Robin switched on a table lamp and drew the curtains.

I sat down on the sofa while Robin went into the kitchen to rummage for a corkscrew and then I heard the clink of glasses as he walked back into the room.

Sitting down next to me he frowned at the wine. "I think that could do with chilling for a bit first.

"I'll go pop it in the fridge."

He got up and I followed him into the galley-style kitchen.

"What did Bill mean" I asked teasing from the doorway of the kitchen "when he asked about me? Just what have you been saying?"

He looked up from the fridge. "I told him that you are bossy." He stood up and closed the fridge door. "Inpatient, sometimes totally impossible and ..." he said as he walked towards me "quite unpredictable. He slowly pulled me toward him, his strong arms encircling my waist. My arms wrapped themselves around his shoulders, my hands stroking the back of his neck. He murmured something, but his words were lost as his mouth covered mine and I abandoned myself to his kisses.

I returned to Cromford House shortly after dawn. Robin drove me back after a long, lingering, and passionate farewell.

I crept back in the house fearing the dogs would hear me and make a noise. Duchess made a fuss, but thankfully remained quiet. The other two dogs were shut in the back of the house and slept on undisturbed.

I softly padded up to my bedroom and sank onto my bed. I was exhausted but my mind and body were still charged with the memory of Robin's touch, and I was unable to sleep. I got off the bed and went for a shower, then put on some clean clothes. I called to Duchess and went out into the garden.

The sun was now rising and had cleared the tops of the trees, stroking the lawns and flower beds with silent golden fingers. The garden was alive with the sound of birdsong and the promise of another hot and sultry day. I headed down towards the rose garden. Sitting down on a bench close to where I had first met Robin, I closed my eyes and breathed in the fresh scent of morning dew and sweet roses. Bees hummed about me on the lavender, eager to start their day's work. Never in my entire life had I felt as contented as I did at that moment, and I knew without any doubt what I had been refusing to accept for some time: I was in love with Robin.

Chapter eleven

Robin and I spent as much time as possible with each other, but as the enchanted evening event drew closer, I found that I spent more time on the telephone than I did in the garden.

Then one week before midsummer, disaster struck: The weather turned wet, windy, and cold.

The weatherman gave out little hope for an improvement and with each advancing day things became gloomier and gloomier. In my excitement, I had forgotten to plan for the weather, and so it was, that one wet and windy afternoon I found myself glued to the telephone desperately trying to source a marquee for my guests to shelter in.

I was in the library; a fire had been lit and Duchess was happily toasting her round pinkish belly in front of it. Outside, rain pattered on the windowpane and trees swayed about in the strong gusty wind, as green leaves were ripped from their branches sending them swirling about in the dull grey sky.

I switched on a table lamp to help ease the gloom and put the telephone directory down on the table with a hearty thump, making Duchess raise her head and look at me in surprise.

I had looked up every supplier listed and had been met with the same reply from each one:

"Everything had been hired out, booked months in advance. Didn't I know that it was the height of the wedding, gala, fete season? Sorry but you have left it too late."

I thanked them all and hung up with a sigh. I was cross with myself for overlooking such an obvious thing and began to doubt my abilities at ever managing a business. I sighed once more and looked out of the window across the wet and windswept garden. The moor was covered in a thick swathe of grey rain-soaked cloud. It clung to the contours of the hills giving it the appearance of a soft velvet ball gown. I hoped that everyone would have the foresight to wear raincoats and bring very large umbrellas.

My stomach began to rumble, and I glanced down at my watch. It was a quarter to five. Well, I thought there was no point on dwelling on the disastrous consequences that the weather may bring and as it was impossible to think of a solution on an empty stomach, I went in search of something to eat.

Janice was away for a couple of days, visiting her sister. She had left some cold meats in the fridge, a casserole to re-heat and a large apple pie with a jug of fresh cream, to tide us over until her return tomorrow. The kitchen was very much Janice's territory. Usually, it was lovely and warm with Janice cooking something in the oven, baking or preparing something delicious to eat. There always seemed to be a kettle whistling away on the stove or someone sat at the table being fed.

Today it was empty, rather cold, and silent and I felt as though I was trespassing on hallowed ground as I entered. Like the rest of the house the kitchen was a little old fashioned, slightly shabby and a little worn. Janice prided herself on not only her cooking abilities, which were second to none but also had her eye on the title of champion cleaner, as a result the kitchen was spotless. Everything had been put away neatly and despite the age and the use of the kitchen everything shone. I wandered over to the aga, my footsteps echoing on the stone tiles of the floor breaking the unfamiliar silence that had invaded the kitchen. I was quite alone.

Miranda was shut up in her office. Raymond had gone off to some farm or other and Simon was out, gamekeeping I presumed and had taken Charlie -Boy and Bracken with him. Even Lillian was out as she had gone into the town to meet some friends and in all probability to do some shopping. She had asked if I would like to go, but I had declined the offer as I had so much work to do here.

I picked up the kettle. I felt a cup of tea and a few biscuits would both cheer me up and bridge the gap before dinner, when I became aware of a cold draught on the back of my legs. I shivered and looked towards the back door, thinking that it blown off the latch in the wind, but it was firmly shut. Then I noticed that the cellar door was ajar.

I put the kettle down next to the sink, still unfilled and went over to shut the door, but saw that the light was on.

"Hello," I called down the stone steps.

There was no reply. "Hello," I called again, only this time much louder.

Perhaps, Lillian was already home and had gone down into the cellar to select a wine for dinner this evening. Lillian was a little hard of hearing although she would never admit it, so I called out loudly: "Lillian" and began to descend the steps. "Hello, Lillian are you down here?"

I reached the bottom step but still there was no answer. I shivered it was very cold down here and I was only wearing a light summer dress and thin cardigan as the library had been very warm on account of the fire.

The cellar had been constructed as a cold store when the house was built. Stone shelves ran along one wall. In the past they would have housed whole bacon joints and salt cured beef, jars of jam, chutneys and pickles and baskets of fruit from the orchard. Now they were home to some half-used pots of paint and odd rolls of left over wallpaper, spare light bulbs and a few boxes of candles, as well as dog food.

There was a stack of logs at the bottom of the stairs, and old baskets and boxes were dotted here and there, that held an odd assortment of things that had not found a home elsewhere in the house. Evidence that Janice did not come down here as it would have been very orderly.

On the opposite wall was a large stone sink. It was quite shallow and had no drainage hole or tap. I believed that it had once been used for preserving meat until more modern and less laborious methods had come along. In front of the sink were the crates of champagne that had been ordered for the enchanted evening and in the sink itself there were the boxes of champagne flutes that I had hired.

I took a few more steps into the cellar my footsteps echoing around.

"Hello" I called. "Anyone here?"

I wasn't sure how far this underground room went; I had only come down once and that was last week when the glasses and champagne had arrived.

I turned a corner a little way ahead and I knew that the wine, and Raymond's prized collection of whiskey was down here, so I thought that perhaps it might be around there, and perhaps that was why Lillian wasn't able to hear me.

It was a little eerie in the cellar. I glanced back up the stairs towards the kitchen door, ignoring the overwhelming urge to rush up the steps and shut the door behind me.

I took a deep breath, walked boldly to the end of the cellar, and rounded the corner.

I fully expected to find Lillian with her glasses perched on the end of her nose scrutinising wine labels, but there were just rows of wooden wine racks holding bottles of various shapes, colours, and sizes. A sudden noise made me abruptly turn.

"Lillian?"

There was a loud bang and a distinctive click, my stomach lurched in fear; the cellar door had slammed shut behind me and the latch had fallen, locking me in

I let out a cry that turned into a scream as the lights went out and I was plunged into total darkness. I tried to calm myself and think rationally. It would be impossible for anyone to hear my cries for help, I had gone quite deep into the cellar and the walls were of a thick construction to keep the cold in and the heat out so that there was little hope of someone in the house would hear me.

I would have to make my way back towards the steps and reach the cellar door, then I could attract someone's attention. I tried hard to visualise my surroundings, but in my momentary panic at being plunged into darkness I had become disoriented. Was the way to the stairs to my left or behind me?

I took a few hesitant steps forward and stumbled into one of the wine racks, I put out my hand to steady myself and felt it wobble. I quickly reached out with my other hand, but I was too close and only knocked it again sending some wine bottles slithering out of their cradles. I could feel the heavy bottles moving forward and toppling, some bounced off me hurting my arms and shoulders. I tried blindly to catch them. I took a step back afraid one would hit my head, but only stumbled into the wine rack behind me, sending another cascade of bottles to the floor. I could hear glass shattering on the floor and the cold wet wine splattering on my legs.

The panic that I had tried to quell now got the better of me and was rising at a frantic pace. I shuffled, in what I thought was away from the wine racks, and in what I hoped to be the direction of the door, paddling through broken glass and puddles of wine. With outstretched and shaking hands I walked into yet another wine rack. More bottles slid from the shelving, tumbling about me to the floor and exploding. I let out a cry as a hot searing pain shot through my leg. With trembling hands, I reached down to the source of the agonising pain, catching my hand on a fragment of broken glass that had embedded itself in the flesh of my calf.

I let out another cry and instinctively ripped the offending shard of glass from my leg, hurling it across the cellar floor. Fright took hold of my senses. I was paralysed with fear, too afraid to move in case more bottles would topple, but too afraid to stay where I was.

My hand began to sting where the jagged edge of the glass had sliced into it. I brought it to my mouth and licked it to ease the pain. It tasted of wine, blood, and my salty tears as they ran down my face. Impatiently, I wiped the tears away, feeling the warm blood smear across my face, as I struggled to think in a calm logical manner. Once more I tried to visualise exactly where I was in the cellar. The throbbing pain in my calf and the warm sticky blood that I could feel trickling down my leg consumed all hope of logical thought: I was going to die. Bleed to death alone in this hell hole of a cellar and no one would find me until it was too late. I let out a sob and resolved in that moment that I was not going to die. Summoning all my courage I took a faltering step forward. The searing pain in my leg caused me to cry out. Glass crunched beneath my feet; wine squelched. But no bottles fell.

Cold beads of sweat began to gather on my face and hands. They ran down my face merging with smeared blood and hot tears. I took another faltering step forward, bracing myself for the agonising pain that each movement brought and the torturous thought that more glass bottles might shatter about me scattering shards of glass like deadly shrapnel.

I shook violently with pain and fear, each step became more and more difficult, and a strange cold began to engulf me. My legs began to buckle unable to support me. I reached out to try and stop myself falling to the ground. I grabbed out at thin air, desperate not to fall on that cold stone floor which was littered with broken glass.

I felt dizzy and lightheaded realising with some relief that I had cleared the wine racks, although the thought was short lived as I collapsed on the floor with a heavy thud and sank into an even blacker darkness of unconsciousness.

I lay on that cold stone floor for how long? minutes, hours, days? I had lost all concept of time. I kept drifting in and out of consciousness. Sometimes I was aware of where I was, and others I was in a horrifying dream.

Gradually, I became aware of a strange sound: faint and far away. There was something familiar about it. I had heard it before, I tried to think, but my mind was muddled lost somewhere between dreams and reality. It grew louder, and more pitiful with each cry. That strange howling invaded my dreams and conscious mind alike and I clung to it believing it was real. As I slid between these two strange worlds a single thought began to take shape in my mind: Duchess.

I called out her name, the words forming on my lips scarcely above a whisper. I tried to crawl forward, but my body refused to move. I lay motionless on the ground, my physical being and will being detached.

Suddenly a shaft of light crossed the cellar floor as the door was opened. I heard the unmistakable sound of a dog's claws scurrying down the steps and voices. The lights came on and I passed out.

Chapter twelve

I awoke in a room filled with bright light and the unmistakable odour of a hospital clinging to it.

Lillian was sitting in a chair beside my bed holding my hand, her face was grey, hollow and tear stained.

"Emily", she said as I opened my eyes. She stroked my forehead like my mother had done when I was a child and was sick or awakened from a bad dream. "You're safe now," she whispered.

"What happened?" I felt weak and groggy, the strain of keeping my eyes open almost too much to bear.

"Raymond found you ... Well, it was Duchess."

Lillian allowed herself a faint smile. "She drove everyone mad yesterday evening. She sat by the cellar door howling. Raymond was trying to read the evening paper and couldn't concentrate. Eventually he lost his temper and swearing hurled the paper to the floor and stormed off saying he was going to sort her out.

"Simon said that you had probably gone out and she was pining for you. He tried to move her out of the kitchen, but she started to bark at him. I thought she was going to bite him. We really had no idea what had got into her. Simon went off to find a muzzle, and Raymond, in an effort to shut her up, just opened the cellar door because she was scratching and whining at it and then going into her full serenade of howls." Lillian paused again, the tears welling up. "Oh Emily ...if we hadn't ... if Simon ..." She stopped, unable to continue, she didn't need to it was clear that if I had been left in that cold dark cellar for much longer that I may have died of hypothermia or more likely bled to death. Either way the outcome would have been the same. I most certainly would have died.

I sank back onto my pillows and closed my eyes; in the space of a few weeks I had my second brush with death. Was this just a coincidence? It was an unsettling thought.

"Why did you go down into the cellar?" Lillian asked.

I opened my eyes to look at her. "I thought you were down there," I croaked, my throat was dry and speaking I found needed effort. "The door was open." I continued slowly. "I thought you were down there choosing some wine for dinner."

"In the dark?"

"The lights ..." I stopped. I was going to say that the lights were on, but then would have implied that someone had deliberately switched them off and locked me in. The only person in the house that afternoon was Miranda.

"Who shut the door?" I asked.

Lillian looked at me enquiringly.

"I don't know. I asked Miranda had she been in the kitchen, and she said no. It was a windy day, she suggested that the wind could have blown it shut and the latch fallen."

Of course, she would say that I thought. My silly idea that Miranda wanted me out of the way was now not so silly, she knew that my cries for help would go unheard. There was no one in the house but her, and the deadly cold of that cellar would soon have taken an effect on me. My clumsiness with the wine racks was just an added bonus. If her intention had only been to frighten me then it had been successful. My mind wandered back to the day at God's Seat. I remembered now how Miranda had come over to my side as I stood with Simon. Had I felt a slight push? Was it possible that she had nudged me then in the hope that I would fall to my death on the rocks below?

I couldn't be sure. What I did know was that she resented me, hated my very presence even and would like nothing better than for me to leave Cromford House. She had even asked after the will was read what would happen should I die. But murder; surely not? Edward Cromford had committed murder – was history repeating itself? I shuddered.

"You're cold," Lillian said concerned.

"No ... No, I'm fine "I lied.

Unaware of the terrible thoughts that were now racing round in my mind Lillian smiled. "The doctors say you will be here for a day or two."

"I can't stay," I wailed. "The enchanted evening." I tried to raise myself up and clamber out of bed, but the effort was too much, and I fell back onto the pillow, tears filling my eyes.

"Emily, you have lost a lot of blood, you need to rest, and you will need to take things easy when you come home too. That gash on your leg was quite savage, you can't risk tearing the stitches."

"Lillian …"

"Doctors' orders," she patted my hand. "Don't worry I'll take care of the enchanted evening, most of the work is done anyway."

So that was it then: my business failed before it had begun. Bankruptcy looming large on the horizon and now I believed that Miranda Maxwell was out to kill me.

Had someone confided these thoughts to me I would have thought that they were suffering from some sort of paranoia and told them not to be so melodramatic over a few silly events that really had no connection. I looked down at my hands, one had an intravenous drip of clear liquid. That's it I thought, a cocktail of drugs that had been administered had given rise to the notion that my life was in danger. I had a severe fright, that's all it was. Nothing to worry about. I was just being silly. I looked at my other hand where a similar drip was attached only this was attached to a bag of blood. This, I thought was no silly matter.

A nurse bustled in. "How's the patient?" she asked. It was a professional courtesy, and she didn't wait for an answer as she put a thermometer under my tongue and began taking my pulse.

She scribbled something down on the clipboard at the bottom of my bed and looked at me thoughtfully.

"You seem a little agitated. Perhaps a sedative to help you to relax and sleep. I'll go and ask the sister."

I agreed, I needed something to quieten the thoughts that were now raging through my head.

She bustled out, returning moments later carrying a stainless-steel dish. She took my hand with the clear drip and began to fumble about. I have always been a little squeamish about needles, so I looked away towards the wall.

"You go home Mum," I heard a voice say. "I'll stay with Emily for a while."

It was Miranda.

I felt a sudden feeling of panic. But the sedative that had been delivered directly into my blood stream was having a rapid effect. My eyes, which had been tired before now struggled to stay open. I desperately clung to Lillian's hand, but my limbs were like dead weights. I wanted to scream out "Don't leave me alone with her." But the effort was too much.

I had become a prisoner in my own body. I felt Lillian gently put my hand on the bed covers and heard the scraping of her chair as she got up to go.

"Goodbye Emily," she whispered, and then her footsteps receded from the room. I heard Miranda move the chair that her mother had been sat on only moments before and smelled the floral notes of her perfume.

I fought with every ounce of strength to keep my eyes open, fearing that once they closed, they would close for good, and I would be committed to the eternal blackness of death. It was no use, the sedative took effect, and I slipped into the blackness any way.

Chapter thirteen

I awoke to a weak and watery sun filtering through the white plastic blinds of the hospital window. Miranda had left and the clock said three thirty p.m. I had slept all through the night and well past the middle of the next day.

A plump nurse with rosy cheeks and a shiny well-scrubbed face was putting some flowers in a vase on the bedside table. She had dark, almost black hair that was pulled back from her face and held tightly in a bun, mimicking her overall roundness.

"Hello," she said cheerily when she saw my eyes open. "A gentleman has brought you some flowers. I told him that you were still sleeping but he said he would wait."

I looked at the flowers, white chrysanthemums, pale pink carnations, and silvery eucalyptus. I smiled; Robin had come to see me.

"Would you like to see him?" the nurse enquired.

I nodded and struggled to sit up. Both drips had been taken from my hands, but my limbs were stiff and painful.

"Here, let me help you," she said leaving the flowers and sliding her hands gently under my arms so that I could sit up. "Boyfriend is he?" she smiled.

"Yes," I said in a dry parched voice.

"Lucky you!" She grinned.

When she had finally sat me up and straightened the bed sheets, she handed me a glass of water. "You've missed lunch, but I can get you some toast if you're hungry."

I took a sip of the water; it was refreshing but not very cold. I licked my lips and took another glug of the water. "Thank you, that would be nice." I put the glass down and tried to smooth my hair which I felt sure looked like a woolly mop.

"Don't worry, you look just fine. I'll tell him to come in and get you that toast."

She bustled out the cheeks of her ample behind wobbling beneath the straining uniform.

The anticipation of seeing Robin soothed away my fears: Miranda Maxwell a murderer: How ridiculous! Yesterday I had just been overwrought, and the drugs like I had initially thought had temporary unhinged me. The terror of being trapped alone in the cold dark cellar had played cruel tricks on my imagination, and the sedative that had been administered had altered my sense of reality.

Oh yes; the whole idea that Miranda was out to kill me was utterly preposterous. That was the voice of reason, the calm logical inner voice that was very easy to listen to in the bright afternoon sunshine of a hospital room. Yet, somewhere in the dark recesses of my mind there was that other little voice. It was just as calm and reasonable as the other voice, and it refused to be shut out and keep quiet. It whispered for me to be on my guard.

The door swung open tearing me away from my deepest thoughts. I looked up eagerly, a bright smile on my face, but my heart sank, and smile faded: it was Simon.

"Emily," he said as he pulled up the chair to the bedside. "How are you? I've brought you some flowers." He nodded towards the vase of flowers.

"Thank you." I mumbled trying to hide my disappointment that he was not Robin.

"I thought they might cheer you up. I would have come sooner, but I was roped into helping Raymond clean up the cellar yesterday. Hell was it a mess, broken glass, blood, and wine everywhere."

"Had many bottles been broken?" I asked trying to block the sound of shattering glass from my memory.

"No, not really, about a dozen or so I'd say."

" Was Raymond cross?"

"No, he was just relieved that you were okay. It really shook him up finding you like that. You had a lucky escape. Mind, he was relieved that his whiskey collection had survived the ordeal.

"Anyway," he said abruptly changing the subject. "How are you feeling?"

"Tired, stiff, and sore! I have no idea how long I'm to be in here and the enchanted evening is only days away," I said glumly.

"Don't fret about that, Lillian has taken over. It's like some sort of military campaign back home. She's had that miserable old sod of a gardener of yours running around like a blue arsed fly. Don't think he's done as much work for years. He was grumbling away that he hasn't had been able to have a fag all morning."

"You mean Tom."

Simon shrugged, "Yeah, think that was his name. And what is that fair haired chap called? Robert?

"Robin." I couldn't help but smile when I said his name.

"Anyway, he and Lillian have been glued together like a couple of conspirators."

The door opened again, and the plump nurse appeared with a tray of hot golden buttery toast and a steaming mug of tea.

"I'd best be going," Simon said taking his cue from the nurse. He stood up and leant forward giving me a light kiss on the cheek. "See you later." And he left.

"I say," the nurse said after Simon had left. "Does that boyfriend of yours have a brother you could introduce me to?"

I felt much better after something to eat and a hot drink and was encouraged by the nurse to get up and walk about. The sooner I was mobile I reasoned the sooner I would be able to leave the hospital.

My leg was very sore where the stitches had been put in and rather stiff. I found that I tired easily and realised that Lillian had been right that I would need to take things easy for a while when I returned home. By the early evening I was back in my bed resting when Robin walked in.

He came silently over to the bed and took me gently in his arms.

He kissed me slowly, my stomach flipping over with each caress of his lips, letting myself slip into him. He pulled away gently. "What am I going to do with you?" he whispered at last.

I shrugged.

He sat up and pushed my hair back from my face. "I wanted to come yesterday when I heard but it was like a battlefield at the house, and this morning Mrs Maxwell told me there was far too much work to be done."

"Yes, Simon told me that she had taken over the event planning."

Robin looked at the flowers. "He brought you those?"

"Yes."

Robin turned towards me, his eyes dull and clouded with concern. "What the hell were you doing in the cellar anyway?"

I told him what I had told Lillian.

"Didn't you think to check that the latch was up? And why in the dark? Bloody hell, Emily ..." he shook his head and raked his fingers through his hair pushing it back from his face "What the hell were you thinking?"

Robins voice was controlled but I could sense the anger behind his words. I was at a loss for what to say. I wanted, needed so badly to comfort him. To tell him the truth, but what was the truth? I had gone down into the cellar and the lights were on. The wind had not blown the door shut but someone had shut that door and turned off the lights. It was plausible that it had been an accident, only strange that no one knew who had shut the door. If I told Robin this it would lead to far too many other questions, and I would run the risk that he would think that I was really in danger, or just paranoid and perhaps mad. No, far better to let him think that I was a fool to go into a cellar with only the light from a kitchen doorway illuminating my way.

So, I remained silent. Robin looked at the vase of flowers again. He cleared his throat, his anger quickly disappearing and said hoarsely, "I should have brought you some flowers."

"It doesn't matter," I said quietly taking his hand." I'm just glad to see you. Let's not quarrel over my silliness."

He looked at me and smiled. "Should I be jealous?" he queried.

"Of whom? Simon?"

He nodded.

"No. Absolutely not," I said forcefully.

He smiled. "Good." He then took my face gently in his hands and kissed me again whispering in a quite husky voice, "if anything should happen to you ..." He kissed me again slowly and deeply before at last drawing away and looking deeply into my eyes. "I love you Emily Cromford," he whispered. "I love you."

"Visiting times over ..." said the plump little nurse as she popped her head round the door, her voice trailing off as she saw me in Robin's arms.

Chapter fourteen

It was Mid Summer's Day when I was finally discharged from the hospital, and it was with mixed feelings that I went back to Cromford House. Lillian and Raymond collected me from the hospital, and Lillian talked endlessly about the arrangements she had made for the evening ahead.

I was of course very grateful to Lillian for all the hard work that she had put in, but I could not shake the feeling of doom that I had for the evening. The weather had at least settled. The gusty winds had dropped and for the moment at least, the rain had stopped, but it was a far cry from the warm sultry evening that I envisaged.

I scarcely listened to Lillian on the way home. I interjected her sentences with answers of yes and no in what I hoped to be the right places. My mind was preoccupied. Thoughts of bankruptcy and failure of the business had now taken second place to a more pressing question: That of Miranda.

I was forced to conclude that I was either losing my mind due to all the pressure that I was under, or that Miranda was trying to kill me. The thought of losing my mind was terrifying enough but the prospect of living with a woman who I believed was trying to kill me, living in fear, and forever looking over my shoulder waiting for her to make her move was equally, if not more so terrifying.

If my business failed and I was forced to sell some of my assets I wondered if Miranda would buy them. I wasn't sure of course, what, if anything I was able to sell and even if this would be enough to satisfy her greed. I would have to be careful. Very careful indeed.

In a curious way the fear and outrage that I felt towards Miranda also gave me a new kind of strength and resolve. Miranda was an intelligent woman, evidently sly and cunning too. I would have to be as equally sly and cunning, if not more so if I were to catch her out. The stakes were much higher for myself, and so I had the edge on the need to succeed. After all, if I was to lose it would cost me my life.

As we rounded the top corner of the drive, I let myself indulge in the surge of pleasure that this vista always brought to me: the view of the house, the dale, and the wilderness of the moor. This was the lost link between my father and myself and I thought stubbornly to myself that I was not going to let it go without a fight.

Then something else caught my attention. It was large, white, and flapping gently in the soft breeze: it was a marquee. I turned to Lillian and gasped, "you found one ... how on earth ...?"

"Oh. I have my contacts," she smiled, tapping the side of her nose in a secret manner.

As I climbed out of the car Duchess came to greet me in what proved to be an emotional reunion as I fought back the tears of love and gratitude towards her.

Janice also rushed out of the house to greet me. She hugged me close, and then scolded me. "You gave us all the fright of our lives!" and then held me at arm's length.

"Oh, look at you, didn't they feed you in that hospital, you're all skin and bone."

"Of course they did" I laughed wiping away a stray tear.

"Uhm ... hospital food. Not fit for man or beast! What you need is some good home cooking down you. Beef and Yorkshire pudding, that'll do the trick."

I knew far better than to disagree with Janice on the subject of food, so I kissed her fondly on the cheek saying, "I'll expect you'll fatten me up in no time!"

She seemed pleased with my answer and nodded her head in acceptance, her face glowing with pride.

The enchanted evening lived up to its name. The weather was cool for late June, but the evening was still and above all dry. Although the moon was not full, the sky was clear, so it cast a beautiful silver glow across the garden.

Lillian's dedication to overseeing the final arrangements for the evening paid off, no one could have guessed the disaster that had struck only days before.

The play was wonderful: the players excelled themselves and were rewarded by a boisterous encore. I became absorbed in the delightful tale of the lovers and the tricks played on them by the queen of the fairies and for an hour or two at least I was able to forget my worries.

During the interval I stood in the marquee eating fresh strawberries and sipping cold champagne. Large bouquets of flowers had been placed around the tent on golden stands. I had ordered the flowers weeks ago and they looked beautiful. Yellow roses, white lilies, and frothy creamy white carnations with large sprays of asparagus ferns and trailing stems of golden variegated ivy mixed among them, cascaded down the legs of the stands like flowing rivers. Fairy lights were strung about to light up the interior of the tent, giving the impression that we were in a sort of fairy tale castle.

The grand finale of the evening was a moonlight stroll about the garden. Guests wandered around the grounds with handheld lanterns and torches. Paths had been specially constructed to lead them from one pixie dell to another. The garden came alive to the sound of laughter and chatter and excited squeals of delight as guests stumbled upon the exquisite fairy scenes that were set up for their amusement.

Lillian and I said goodbye to our guests shortly after midnight. We were thanked profusely for the evening and received many enquiries as to when our next event would be.

"Well," said Lillian as the last of the guests disappeared down the long winding drive. "I think it's safe to say that that was a raving success." She turned and took my hand in hers. "Mum would have been so proud of her garden tonight." She kissed me tenderly on the forehead. "Good night, Emily." And she wandered off in the direction of the house.

There was a lot of clearing up to do but it could all wait until the morning. I looked about me, the garden was dark and deserted. I smiled to myself. I loved the garden when it was like this, all silent and ready to divulge its secrets to me. Robin came to stand by my side with a glass of champagne in each hand. "A toast," he said, "to your success."

"No. A toast to our success," I corrected him and took the glass from his outstretched hand.

We each took a sip and then smiling he took my other hand and gently led me down the garden.

We wandered silently together sipping champagne as we walked past a lighted fairy waterfall and the herbaceous borders where moths were gorging themselves on the sweet nectar of the flowers. I felt as though I was in Shakespeare's play. I was Helena and Robin my Demetrius. Two lovers, secretly meeting in a woodland glade on Mid- Summer's Eve.

The garden was still. The silence was only broken by the soft hooting of an owl and the muffled stirrings of creatures in the undergrowth. The moon softly caressed each tree, bush and sleeping flower. The sky was a dark velvet blue, studded with glistening stars. Silvery grey shadows cast themselves across smooth pewter-coloured lawns and the tips of conifer trees glowed like silver candles.

Robin led me deeper into the garden. Soon we had left all the pixies, sprites, and fairy dells behind and reached the summer house where the garden merged with the orchard.

Inside he had placed lighted candles and scattered rugs and cushions on the floor. As we entered, he took me in his arms and placed our now empty glasses on a side table where an ice bucket contained an unopened bottle of champagne. He pulled me towards him, and we fell together to the floor among the cushions and blankets. We made love, sipped champagne, and listened to the melody of the night on that most enchanted of enchanted evenings.

Chapter fifteen

The morning after the enchanted evening the skies darkened again, and it rained heavily for what seemed like days on end. Today, however there had been a brief respite in the weather and I was sitting by the lily pond on the upper terrace. Robin was beside me weeding one of the flower beds and although rather humid the sun was hidden behind misty clouds of pale grey.

My wounds were healing well but I was of little use in the garden. The dressings had come off, but it would be a while longer before the stitches were to be taken out. The wound on my leg was now a horrible mix of purple and a lurid yellowy-green colour. It was not painful although the stitches had become tight and itchy.

"One good thing about all this rain," Robin said as he hoed between the plants, "is that it cuts down the need for watering."

I looked up from the pond where I had been watching a large golden Koi carp struggling to eat a root of a plant mistaking it for a fat juicy worm.

"If the new pond system had been dug it would be full now," I said.

"Overflowing more like," he grunted. "I can't remember a wetter June. When are the contractors due to start?"

"Middle of next week, but I don't know if the ground will be too wet. I suppose that it has taken this long, another few weeks won't make that much of a difference."

He nodded. "I just hope all the hard landscaping is done by the start of October so we can get planting done before winter sets in. I'm hoping that the frogs will find the ponds next spring and give us a hand with this slug problem." Robin bent down and picked up a bedraggled leaf.

"Have you seen what they have done to this Hosta?" He held up what should have been a large fleshy leaf of vivid green striped with gold, it now hung in tatters and was covered in slime and mud. "This year has been a slug heaven."

"You really do say the most romantic things to a girl," I teased.

He smiled. "Mrs Maxwell wants you."

"What?"

"Mrs Maxwell," he pointed towards the French windows on the house.

"Oh," I said turning around to see Lillian standing at the window.

"Have you got a minute?" she mouthed silently to me.

I nodded to her to say yes and then said to Robin, "I'll go and see what she wants. Will I see you tonight?"

He stopped hoeing between the plants again. "Sorry Emily, I have something planned for this evening."

"That's okay," I said in a chirpy voice to hide my disappointment. "I'll catch up with you tomorrow." I got up from where I was sitting and walked towards the house.

Lillian opened the French doors, and I took off my shoes laying them carefully on the mat by the door. Duchess padded in behind me leaving a faint but noticeable trail of paw prints across the carpet. I made a mental note to remove them before Janice saw them.

"You and Robin seem to have become rather fond of each other," Lillian observed as she closed the door behind me.

"Yes, we have become quite good friends," I said rather evasively.

"Friends!" She raised an eyebrow at me. "I think that perhaps you are a little more than just friends."

"Well." I began blushing.

"Don't worry Emily," she said. "I'm not Janice and going to broadcast the fact!"

We laughed and she turned to look out of the window watching Robin break off from his work for a few moments as he studied a nearby thrush demolishing a snail's shell. "Mum liked him," she said. "She thought that he was a true gentleman, both in his manner and character."

"Yes," I said behind her, "he is," thinking about his quiet and tender ways.

Lillian turned and went to sit in one of the chairs by the fire. Although it was now almost the beginning of July a small fire had been lit as it felt rather damp and chilly in the room, it also helped to lift the mood on the dull day.

"What did you want with me, Lillian?" I asked sitting in the opposite chair to her.

"Well," she said. She looked quite animated, her eyes sparkling. I had seen that look before.

"Lillian," I said slowly, "have you been investigating again?"

"Well, yes," she grinned, "I've been to see a friend of mine. She used to work for a law firm – many years ago now though, but I thought she might be able to help me find out some more information."

"You are a dark horse, Lillian!"

"I know," she chuckled.

"Was she shocked when you told her about Edward?"

"No, she was more intrigued than shocked. Rosie and I go back a long way. We were at college together. She's a grandmother now to two adorable youngsters ..."

"Was she able to help?" I butted in. Lillian tended to ramble, and I was eager to know what she had learnt and not the life history of Rosie which I knew was about to follow.

"Yes," Lillian said quite unperturbed to be cut off mid-sentence. "We didn't really discover much else about Edward Cromford, so she suggested that we investigate the victims. The poor dead girl had worked in Cromford House but had left about four months prior to her death."

I sat back in my chair. "So, Edward would have known her and ... possibly quite well!"

"Quite well?" Lillian questioned.

I sighed. "The girl was pregnant, wasn't she? Maybe the baby was Edward's?"

Lillian went very quiet thinking. "Possibility, hadn't thought of that."

"What else did you find out about her?"

"She came from the northeast of England and lived at Cromford House during her employment which lasted about eighteen months."

"So, my theory then, that Edward was perhaps the father of the baby could be correct?"

"Yes," she grimaced. "I very much suppose that it could, and that he was …" She shuddered. "What a dreadful thought!"

"I know, and the other girl?"

"Evelyn Slater. We already knew she worked at Cromford House, she was a daily and lived in the village with her mother and younger brother. And …" the excitement creeping back into Lillian's voice again. "Her brother lives in the village, in one of our properties as it happens. His name is William Slater. Here," she handed me a slip of paper. "This is his address. I think that we should pay him a visit. He's an old man now, but I'm sure he will remember what actually happened."

I nodded and spoke. "It's not going to be a pleasant visit though. I expect that even after these years that the disappearance of his sister is going to be something of a difficult subject."

A thought suddenly occurred to me. "Lillian, do you suppose that Roberta had spoken to him and maybe that is why she changed her will?"

"You mean he told Mum that Edward was innocent?"

"Yes, why not."

She sat back in her chair and shook her head slowly. "Oh, Emily I would so like to believe that but look at all the evidence against Edward. I think Mum changed her will because she thought it was the right thing to do."

Lillian sighed, her eyes losing all their sparkle. "As you get older," she said softly, "your past can become a burden. There is no time to reflect in your youth while you're in the thick of things. Then, gradually as life slows down you start to see the cracks and feel the urge to smooth them out before it's too late. Mum had a strong sense of justice, perhaps she was tired of punishing her brother and wanted to forgive him, and the only way to do that was to let his children have a share in what he should have had."

I was quiet for a while thinking about what she had said. It was all so sad. In conversations with people about Roberta I had discovered that she was respected and very well liked for her fairness and strength of character. Lillian's speculation made sense and I could well understand the reasoning behind Roberta's gift to me.

I looked down at the name and address on the piece of paper that Lillian had handed me and felt my heart stop.

William Slater
12 River View Lane

Evelyn's brother lived in the same row of cottages as Robin. He was the old man that I had seen on the river and who Robin was friendly with. Bill of course being a shortened version of William.

I looked out of the window. It had started to rain again, and Robin had gone. The rain drops slithered down the panes of glass, merging with each other forming trickles that gathered speed and became miniature rivers. I could feel the thumping of my heart in my chest and my mind began to race.

What if Bill were to tell Robin the sordid details about my grandfather? Bill had known who I was the first time we met. I was sure that those old, but keen eyes of his knew that Robin and I were lovers. If he were to tell Robin about Edward would Robin think that I had deliberately concealed my past from him? I had no idea how he would react. Robin was such a gentle, trusting soul that I feared it would destroy our relationship. There was only one thing for me to do. I must go and speak to Bill. I had to find out the truth no matter how unpleasant it might be and plead with him not to tell Robin. I would have to see him soon.

"I'll go and speak to William Slater" I heard myself say in a far-off voice.

Chapter sixteen

I was confined to the house for the rest of the afternoon as it continued to rain heavily, and a thick fog-like mist had developed devouring the outside world.

I hated days like these. The house felt like a prison, the walls closing in around me, making me feel claustrophobic. I wondered if my relationship with Miranda had been different then would I have felt like this? The constant vigilance that I felt I had to exercise when I was in the house with Miranda, always looking over my shoulder to see where she was, had, I believe started to have a marked effect on my nerves. I was uncertain how long I would be able to endure this deadly game of cat and mouse that I had unwittingly started to play.

I retired to the library after lunch to go over the accounts and to start some planning for my next up and coming events. Concentration was difficult, the thoughts of Bill were going round in my head and my mind kept wandering off to the imagined conversation that I would have with him.

I stared at the figures on the paper, they certainly looked a lot healthier than they had done a month or two ago. Still, even this and the prospect of holding other events failed to lighten the melancholic mood that had descended upon me, just like the wet miserable weather that had descended on the surrounding countryside.

Time dragged: the clock seemed to tick more loudly than usual. The rain drummed on the windowpane and Duchess was softly snoring by the fire. The house was still and silent.

Suddenly, about mid-afternoon, the silence was broken. The other dogs in the house began to bark excitedly, waking Duchess, who lifted her head to see what the commotion was about. There were raised, agitated voices and running footsteps. Doors slammed and the vehicles parked outside were fired up. I got up and looked out of the window to see Raymond and Simon with several other men who worked on the estate drive off at some speed down the driveway, leaving a spray of mist in their wake. I went out into the hallway to see if I could find out what was happening when I ran straight into Miranda.

I was startled to see her. I had thought that she was in her office at the opposite end of the house and that I was safe in the library.

"What are you doing here?" I demanded of her.

She looked at me puzzled. "The river has burst its banks. Dad and the others have been called out to assist at one of the farms to move the livestock to higher ground away from the flood waters.

"That doesn't answer my question." I snapped.

Miranda looked taken aback at my abrupt, rude manner, murmured. "I was on my way to the kitchen for a coffee. Would you like one?"

I stared at her. I wanted to scream in her face. "I bet you were, and what would you put in my coffee -- rat poison?" I slammed the library door in her face.

I leant against the door my heart thumping loudly in my chest, my breathing deep and uneven. I peered through the keyhole at Miranda who looked bewildered, a perplexed expression on her face at my irrational outburst. She turned and walked away in the direction of the kitchen, her heels gently tapping down the hallway.

Satisfied that she had gone, I let myself relax and slithered down the door into a crumpled heap at the bottom.

I had become irritable and jumpy. My nerves were raw. I was tired, so very, very tired but I found that when I did sleep, I still woke unrefreshed and unrested. Peace eluded me. I needed to escape, but where could I run?

Duchess came over to see me, sensing that something was wrong. I reached out to touch her soft fur and let the tears that I had held back so long flow unhindered. She lay down beside me and comforted me as I wept.

I sat there for some time, even after the tears had stopped and my face had become hot, dry, and sticky. I gazed into space unwilling to move, with Duchess resting her head on my lap. Then it came to me. I knew what I must do. I would tell Robin. I would put my trust in him and tell him my fears about Miranda. If he thought I was insane, then perhaps at least I would not have to face it alone. There would be no more secrets between us, and that of course meant that I would have to tell him about Edward Cromford. I picked up myself mentally and physically off the floor. I would go and see Bill today: Right now in fact, and find out the truth about my grandfather.

It was late afternoon when I silently crept out of the house, the rain had stopped and there was just a light drizzle. I had left a contented Duchess in the kitchen. Janice was roasting some chickens for our supper and the delicious mouth-watering aroma of the roasting birds was permeating the house. Duchess was lying in her basket, carefully observing the activities that went with the making of a meal, patiently waiting for the golden chickens to come out of the oven to rest in the hope that one of them, by chance might accidently leap to the floor and need rescue.

The quickest way to Bill's cottage was through the garden and along the river. It would be twice as long by the road. There would be very little traffic, but as there was no footpath, I would still need to beware of passing vehicles. With the river in full spate, I knew that the sensible option would be the road, but I was consumed by this urgent, selfish need to discover the truth and unburden myself from the torments that plagued my mind. So, I headed down the garden towards the river.

The soothing scent of the damp earth and wet foliage began to weave its magic spell around me and calm my overwrought mind. As I reached the orchard the drizzle stopped, and a gentle wind started up. It lightly touched the leaves of the trees and sent showers of collected rain drops to the ground in silver cascades. Blooms, on long slender stems, quivered and shook the surplus water from their petals. A blackbird began to sing, its cheerful melody echoing around the garden, while a family of bluetits flitted from tree to tree in search of bedraggled insects, and close by, the shrill call of a tiny wren began declaring that the rain had at last stopped.

I reached the woodland which bordered the garden quickly. Usually, I meandered my way along stopping to look at this plant, or that, admiring the landscape or the form of a tree. But today I had only one goal in my mind and that was to reach Bill's as quickly as possible. Even the dull ache in my leg did not impede my progress.

The thick canopy of leaves made it seem dark, almost nighttime in the wood. Already I could hear the river gushing as it raced angrily downstream. The air was filled with the scent of wild garlic, always much stronger when the weather was damp – and because of the copious amounts of water in the recent weeks it had flowered profusely. The woodland floor was carpeted with its white pom- pom like flowers which shone like stars in the gloom.

In several places the river was freely flowing along the footpath forcing me to go around on a different route. The river moved along in a smooth, rapid undulating motion. Debris that had been caught further upstream was swept along at some speed by the strong current and the bank on the other side of the river had been breached, with water spreading up into the fields.

I began to question whether I should have come this way at all. The dull ache in my leg was progressively getting worse and I knew that the path would get more strenuous further on. Still, I was consumed with this sense of urgency. If I were to turn back now it would take me another hour, possibly two to reach Bill's. No, I ignored my common sense and continued down the river towards the narrowest point and the most treacherous: The Striddings.

The closer I got to The Striddings the louder the river became, until it was a deafening roar that consumed all other sounds. There must have been thousands upon thousands of gallons of water being channelled into that narrow course way.

The river had become a ferocious beast, resenting the cage-like constraints of the surrounding terrain. It raged and spat at the rocks, fighting to regain its freedom. The water ran black. Foam and spray were flung into the air above, branches from trees that had been ripped away further upstream and had ridden on the waves had now been sucked under by the raging torrent as it pummelled on the rocks below. Wave upon wave of water pounded the riverbank, battering it, scouring the earth below, stripping it of its soil and exposing bare tree roots.

The wide footpath was flooded. The red metal pole of the life ring was submerged up to its belly. The life ring was inaccessible, but I doubt that if anyone was to fall into those raging waters, they would survive long enough to grasp a thrown life ring. I wondered how long the pole would survive this brutal battering that it was now receiving,

I scrambled up onto the higher path, which was wet, muddy, and dangerously slippery. I struggled along, slipping and sliding. I too, was now soaked as each new breath of wind brought cascades of water down on me from the treetops. With cold wet hands I clung onto tree trunks, branches, tufts of grass; anything to pull myself along and to steady myself.

The pain in my leg intensified and became more acute with each step and I became increasingly afraid that I would either become stranded on this muddy embankment or that I would topple into the raging waters below.

At last, the path became a little wider and less steep, as it began to veer away from the river, and I breathed a sigh of relief as the meadow and the little row of cottages where Bill lives came into sight.

As I left the wood and crossed the meadow, the sky looked a little more settled. Breaks had begun to appear in the thick grey clouds and here and there were patches of dull blue. I wasn't sure of the time, I had left my watch on the dressing table, but I guessed that it was around seven p.m. It would still give me time to get back home before the evening closed in as it was around ten before the sun set at this time of year.

I hurried as fast as my leg would allow across the meadow and winced as I climbed the stile at the end. Still, I did not stop, fuelled as I was by this compelling desire for knowledge, the knowledge of a past that intertwined with my present and had the power to shape my future, and relieve me of my inner torment.

I scurried along the lane. I passed Robin's house, pulling my hood up and almost over my face in fear that he might see me and headed straight up Bill's path. With a pounding heart, both from the exertion of the walk and apprehension I took a deep breath and knocked forcefully on the door.

There was a barking from inside, the sound of footsteps, and a voice: "All right Bess, good girl."

The door opened.

Everything that I had planned to say went out of my head and instead I blurted out. "I have come to ask you about Edward Cromford; and Evelyn."

Bill looked at me for what seemed like an eternity and then said. "I wondered when you would."

Chapter seventeen

"Not the sort of day to be taking a stroll, is it?" Bill said wryly as I struggled to take off my boots in the doorway. "Here, let me help you," he said as he watched me wrestle with a muddy boot. He brought a wooden stool and helped me to sit down, then taking the boot firmly in his hand he tugged it free.

"Thank you," I said as he handed me a clean, but old and faded towel to dry my face and hands. I took off my coat and rubbed my wet hair with the towel.

"You go and sit yourself down by the fire," he said taking my coat and laying it out to dry. "I'll go and make a hot drink."

As he ambled off towards the kitchen, I looked around the tiny front room. The curtains had already been drawn to shut out the murky grey, although it was still reasonably light outside and a table lamp had been lit giving the room a welcoming cosy glow. I went to sit by the log-burning stove. Bess followed and made a quiet fuss of me as I sat down.

Bill returned with two steaming mugs of tea, handed me one and told Bess to go and lie in her bed.

We sat facing one another in front of the fire. Bill studied me closely, a faint smile on his lips and I wondered if I'd done the right thing in coming here at all.

I took a sip of my tea, pausing for time before launching into the speech that I had been rehearsing all afternoon in my head, but now the moment had arrived I was at a loss for what to say.

I took another slurp of tea; it was far too sweet and milky for me, but I drank it any way, stalling for time and thinking that it would just be better to just ask what I desperately needed to know. And that was: did my grandfather murder those two girls?

Bill got up and went over to the sideboard, opened a door, and pulled out a tin of shortbread biscuits. He sat down opposite me again and took the lid off the tin. He held out the tin to me, I was about to refuse a biscuit, when I realised, to my surprise that the contents of the tin were not creamy yellow and strewn with sugar, but an odd assortment of photographs and letters.

I took the tin from him and took out the topmost photograph. It was black and white, cracked and a little torn, curling around the edges, but I recognized the setting at once: it was Cromford House.

There was a group of people standing on the steps that led up to the front door. It must have been taken in the late spring because the wisteria that was cascading over the front of the house was in full bloom. It was much smaller than it was today only reaching up above the front door on long slender stems. Now those same stems were as thick as tree trunks, twisted and gnarled with age and spanned the full length of the house reaching the upper floor.

The people in the photograph were lined up in a formal fashion, some were wearing servants' uniforms, the women in long black dresses and frilly aprons and caps, and the men in smart suits with white shirts and starched collars.

"That's Edward Cromford," Bill said pointing to a man close to the centre of the group. He was very tall and handsome with a moustache and wavy hair that I guessed was of a similar colour to Lillian's when she had been young. "And you want to know if he murdered my sister – and that other young girl."

I looked up sharply away from the photo and into Bill's watery old eyes.

"Well, let's get this straight," he said abruptly. "Edward Cromford was a lot of things. He was a gambler, liked his drink and was probably a little too fond of the ladies, but he was no murderer."

"How can you be sure?" I gasped, completely taken aback by his forceful statement, "I mean ... all the evidence!"

"I have all the evidence I need," he said losing all trace of the ferocity that he had displayed earlier and then said in a soft voice, "I knew that I should have spoken up at the time, but I was only a lad and our Evie made me promise. Any road, I thought no harm would come of it to say nowt." He shrugged. "I was wrong."

"You mean – you knew ! You knew all that time he was innocent, and you just kept quiet!"

I found it incredulous that he had remained silent about such a thing. I was angry, angry that he had kept the truth hidden and let everyone believe that Edward was guilty of murder.

"And the family," I demanded, my fury growing. "What about the rift that it caused within the family?"

"I know, I know," Bill said holding up his hands in order to defend himself from my words.

I glared at him.

"Don't look at me like that," he said tartly. "Things aren't always what they seem, and never as simple and straightforward as we would like."

He sat back in his chair and frowned. "Edward and Evelyn were lovers. It was considered wrong in those days that the classes should mix, and it would have certainly enraged Edward's father, not to mention Mum."

He gave a weary sigh, and then continued. "Edward was engaged to be married to a daughter of a business associate of his father. I don't know the details, but I gathered that there was some sort of financial reward, because the local gossip was that James Cromford, your great grandfather, had lost rather heavily on the stock market. I also suspect that Edward had run up a fair amount in gambling debts and that his creditors knowing of his father's financial problems would be wanting to collect their money. If Edward were to marry there would have been a large dowry and it would have settled the debts of both father and son. Problem was Edward loved Evelyn."

"How can you be so sure he was innocent? I mean, just because you say that he loved her doesn't mean that he didn't murder her. Perhaps ..." I said now warming to my new theory. "The other girl knew of the affair and was threatening to blackmail Edward. The lure of money can be an extremely powerful motive." I felt a shiver creep down my spine as I spoke those words as the image of Miranda came into my thoughts. Oh yes, I thought; money and the greed it generates in some people can be a very powerful motive indeed.

"Because," Bill continued, "the night that the young girl was killed, Edward was with Evelyn." He paused and took a mouthful of tea. "I was in the orchard at Cromford House stealing apples. I used to go up at night and Mam would make apple crumble the next day!" he chuckled. "Any road. I heard voices in the summer house, and I recognized them as our Evelyn's and Edwards: They were planning to elope. I got a bit careless with my eavesdropping and they heard me. Evelyn gave me a good clout for spying on her, and then another for pinching apples." He grinned and rubbed his face as he remembered the force of the clout.

"They made me swear to keep what I had just heard a secret. You see Evelyn would have needed to have consent to be married and they told me that the authorities would prosecute if they did. I don't know if it were true or not, but I believed them. Any road, if they had stayed here, they would never have been able to marry, James Cromford would have made sure of that. Edward would have been forced to marry that other lass and Evelyn would have lost her job and we would have been turfed out of the house and village. No, they had to run away. It was just bad timing on their part.

So, you see, I know for a fact that Edward did not kill Evelyn any more than he could have strangled that other poor girl."

"But ... when the manhunt was launched ... your mother. surely it would have been better for her to know that her daughter was safe?"

"Aye, broke my heart to see Mam like that. I did try to tell her, but I was in deep with the lie then. And I figured that it would only be a short time before they could marry."

"Did Evelyn contact your mother? Did she ever know?"

"No." Bill said shaking his head sadly. "Mam caught the influenza shortly afterwards and died. I think it was grief that really killed her. I was angry with Evie for a long time but that was because I knew that I was also to blame."

"Evelyn never got in touch with you?"

"She may have tried, but I wouldn't have been that easy to find. After Mam died, I was sent to a children's home in south Yorkshire. I had no other family so there wasn't a choice. And from there I was fostered by a family in Doncaster. Once the war broke out it would have made things even more difficult. I never tried to find her either, I had no idea where they had gone." He shrugged, "It was just the way things were."

"I am sorry," I said saddened, now realising how the illicit love affair had affected the lives of so many people. I was relieved that Edward was innocent, but this of course then raised another question that had puzzled everyone for months: Why had Roberta changed her will?

"Did you tell Roberta about her brother?"

He got up and opened the front of the stove and threw on another log. Bess lifted her head, and he reached out to stroke her saying something softly then he looked at me. "I didn't seek her out if that's what you're asking; but yes, I did tell her, and it was purely accidental." He sat back down in his chair with a heavy thud.

"I had been back in the village about a month, and decided it was time that I laid some ghosts to rest. I went up to the church where my mam is buried. I was stood at the entrance gates hesitating; I wasn't sure how I felt, it had been a long time ago when I was last there. A lady came by, she had a dog with her; that lab that seems to be fond of you. She stopped and remarked on the lovely day and then asked if I was a visitor. I said no and she mistook my hesitation by the gates for reading the times of the church services. She passed a comment on how boring they had become in the last year because of the new reverend and said he should hire himself out to insomniacs as it would improve the church funds no end.

She laughed, and in that instant, I knew who she was. She still had the fire of the young Roberta. Always laughing and finding humour in the most mundane of things. And making inappropriate comments. I didn't let on who I was though. Then she mentioned a reverend that had been at the church in her youth and how lively and entertaining his sermons had been. I said I remembered him, and my silly remark led to me telling her who I was. We went for a coffee, and I told her what I have told you now. Her brother was not guilty.

I sat and listened, intrigued, everything starting to fall into place. "Well, it seems," I said, "that your chance encounter led Roberta to change her will in favour of me!"

Bill shrugged and laughed softly.

"If what you say is true though, "I said, "Evelyn and Edward must have gone to Ireland. That's where my father was born. But they must have gone their separate ways shortly after arriving there though because Mr Walker has a copy of my father's birth certificate and his mother's name was a lady named Judith."

Bill shook his head slowly. "No, they didn't part. Our mother's middle name was Judith. She must have changed her name, taken on a new identity to make it harder for anyone to find her."

Suddenly he smiled. "You look like her you know. It's the eyes; the hair too, but noticeably the eyes, a deep shade of blue; just like the wild bluebells."

"Who, what?" I asked bewildered.

"Our Evie of course!" He chuckled. "That day I first saw you by the river coming through the trees, thought you were her for a second, come to tell me off for poaching."

"You mean ..." I said slowly, the meaning of what he had just said sinking in. I looked down towards the photograph again. At the edge of the group was a young servant girl. She had thick, dark wavy hair that despite all the pins she had tried to secure it with was still trying to escape. She was smiling brightly, her face animated and it bore a striking similarity to my own.

"Evelyn's your grandmother." He laughed.

Chapter eighteen

It was still daylight when I left Bill's; but only just. The rain had been swept away by strong gusty winds and I was wrapped up in my still damp coat to keep out its chill. I scurried along the lane away from Bill's. I was giddy with excitement and eager to share my newfound knowledge with Lillian. I hesitated by Robin's house; should I call in now and tell him all my secrets, that only a few hours ago had seemed to be so important? No, I decided, I would tell him first thing tomorrow. Anyway, his house showed no signs of life, and then I remembered that he had said he was busy tonight. Besides, the walk and the time with Bill had somehow put my fears into perspective. The desperate urgency that I had felt only a few hours previously had dulled. I was still fearful of Miranda, but I felt calmer in myself.

The moon had risen. Pale, wispy clouds were scurrying across its face so that it glowed dimly in the sky like a mother of pearl shell under the ripples of a cold grey sea.

I reached the stile that led across the meadow towards the river and paused. My leg was rested but I was reluctant to repeat the treacherous journey that I had undergone. I had been a fool to come that way. Far safer I thought to take the long route home along the road.

I hadn't walked very far when a Land Rover pulled up beside me. I recognised it at once to be Simon's.

"Emily!" he said in surprise as he leaned over the passenger seat and slid the window open. "What an earth are you doing here?"

I had no intention of telling Simon my reason. Perhaps he would think that I had been to see Robin. "I came out for a walk."

He raised a quizzical eyebrow at my response. The knowledge that Edward was innocent of murder and the elation that Evelyn was my grandmother had made me feel as lightheaded and intoxicated as though I had a good glug of sweet wine. I laughed at him and said, "I could ask you the same question."

A flash of annoyance crossed his handsome features. Simon didn't like to be questioned over his activities and my flippant tone only served to irritate him.

"I've been down the Simpsons' place," he said. "They've been hit hard by the floodwater and needed help to move the livestock. Raymond's still down there now. The water is rising fast and threatening some of the outbuildings. I'm off now to some of the other low-lying farms to see how they're coping."

"Yes, the river had already burst its banks when I came down earlier."

Simon stared at me. "What?" he said in disbelief. "You came down via the Striddings?"

I nodded.

"Of all the stupid ... irresponsible ...dumb ..." He stopped, a strange thoughtful look entered his eyes and then his attitude changed. "It is spectacular when it's like that though, don't you think? All that power. The raw energy of the water ... surging, violent, so out of control. Come on, let's go and take a look."

"What now?"

"Yes, right now!"

He swiftly manoeuvred the Land Rover onto the grass verge up ahead of me and switched off the engine.

"But you just said it was treacherous," I said as he came to stand beside me.

"It is, but I don't intend to get so close, I just want to go and take a look."

I reluctantly followed him the short distance down the road towards the stile.

We crossed the meadow, Simon walking so fast I had to jog to keep up with him.

"Simon, "I called out. "My leg. you're going too fast ... slow down!" but he ignored me.

The roar of the river could already be heard, it was far louder than when I had first come past, and I knew that it had become more swollen. The last of the daylight faded away as we entered the gloom of the woodland and it felt as though night-time had engulfed us.

Simon shouted above the roar of the river; "We're almost there," and reached out and took my hand.

Through the dim light that had managed to penetrate the thick canopy of leaves I could see the river as a swirling mass of glistening black.

Still walking faster than comfortable for my leg and with Simon's firm hold of my hand we marched towards the Striddings.

Very soon we came to the Striddings. The pole for the life ring swayed violently with the brute force of the water. The ring had already been ripped off and was caught on a tree branch on the other side of the bank, it was receiving a severe beating until the branch it was caught on finally cracked and was sent spinning away down river. The life ring tore free and went swirling along with the other debris that was strewn across the water's surface: twigs, branches, planks of wood, plastic bottles, and hundreds of leaves. Then a dead sheep swept past. Battered and beaten by the river, her two drowned lambs trailed behind her. I shuddered and turned away at the sight.

I don't know if it was the dark and unfamiliar terrain of the wood, the sound of the violent gushing water or the sight of those pitiful creatures, but a strange sense of foreboding stole over me and I wanted to flee from the river, the wood and Simon.

"NO!" I shouted at Simon and abruptly stopped.

Simon turned round and looked at me, his eyes gleaming. His hand tightened its grip on mine, and he pulled me towards him. "Come on" he said gruffly.

"NO!" I shouted again at him. "Let me go, you're hurting me."

I struggled to free myself from his tight grasp, but his grip was far too strong for me, my shouts became screams of terror as I began to feel the cold wet grasp of the river surging over my feet and reaching up over my legs. Simon brutally pulled me further round into the river and then released me. I staggered and slipped, then another vice-like grip took hold of me by the legs.

They were like Simon's hands only colder and stronger and were dragging me down towards them. They clawed at my thighs, my waist, pulled my shoulders and slapped my face as I felt myself fall into the frenzied river.

I grasped at the exposed tree roots to stop myself being sucked under by the torrent. They were slimy and cold with mud and foam, and they cut into the flesh of my hands but all I could do was cling. The river laughed at me as I screamed, I had become its latest plaything. It would rip my body from its banks and snap me in two as surely and as easily as I could snap a flower from its stem.

I grappled with the tree roots and struggled to keep myself above the water. A movement on the riverbank attracted my attention. Had someone been in the trees watching Simon and me? The figure swiftly moved forwards towards me, their fair hair shining like a beacon in the gloom. Miranda! It had to be Miranda.

With my life now most certainly over as I felt all strength ebb away from my limbs, time seemed to slow down. A rare clarity of thought struck me. Simon and Miranda were in this together. He was her accomplice to murder. How could I have not seen it before?

My death would be recorded as a misfortunate accident, and I would become just another victim of the river.

An enquiry would reveal that I had been to Bill's that evening and had taken the short cut back to Cromford House along the river, and that I had most probably stumbled or slipped into the river and then drowned like so many before me. Death by misadventure they call it. No one would ever suspect foul play.

What share in the estate had Miranda bribed Simon with? Had she been forced to include him in her schemes at her failed attempt to rid herself of me at God's Seat? For I was certain now that day I had been deliberately pushed with the intent to kill me.

It would have been possible for either one of them to lock me in the cellar that day, and like now they would have been able to fabricate alibis for one another and then later congratulate themselves over their cleverness. Perhaps sipping champagne and gloating over their victory together.

I felt sick to the stomach. I had played right into their hands, creating the perfect accident. I felt my hands slip on the tree roots as my grip loosened through exhaustion. I felt no fear only an overwhelming sadness for everything that might have been. I thought of Robin and my mother, I didn't want to leave them, but the river was too powerful a match for me.

Suddenly a violent pain shot through my shoulder as I felt it pop from the socket, my head jerked backwards forcing me to look straight up into a wet, mud-covered face with strands of blonde hair clinging to it. Miranda was going to finish me off here and now, the river wasn't doing the job fast enough for her, but it wasn't Miranda's triumphant face that I looked upon: It was Robin's.

A dull pain exploded in my head as something heavy glanced of the side of it and a darkness engulfed me.

Chapter nineteen

I was drifting, drifting downstream. The water was slow and glass like. I could see the amber coloured pebbles of the riverbed. Leaves swirled and spiralled past, caught up in the eddies and currents of the water. I was weightless, suspended in time, cocooned in an eerie silence. I was no longer afraid, I let the river take me, accepting the peace it offered and gladly surrendering myself to its gentle embrace.

"Emily," a voice broke into my strange silent world. It was close by. I tried to turn my head towards it.

"Emily." It whispered again.

My eyes were heavy, so very heavy, I tried slowly, ever so slowly to open them.

An outline, blurred at first, started to take shape, and I began to focus on the face that I had grown to love.

"Emily," Robin said again, and reached out to touch me.

I felt myself recoil in horror as the memory of clinging to tree roots and the savagery of the water, entered my mind. But I was alive. Or was I? Was this also a dream?

"Emily, you're safe now." His voice was barely above a whisper and his eyebrows had knitted together in a look of concern.

I closed my eyes, my head ached, my body felt battered and bruised. I was confused, so very, very confused.

Where was I? What had happened? I tried to think clearly: Go over the events again in my mind, the roar of the river. My screams of terror, Simon's roughness, and Miranda. Where was Miranda? But it wasn't Miranda, it was Robin that I saw. He was the figure in the woodland, and the one stood by the water's edge, kneeling by the river as I clung on for my life.

I squeezed my eyes shut, I didn't want these memories, I wanted them to go away. I wanted everything to go away.

"Emily," he spoke again, and I felt his hand caress my cheek as hot tears started to trickle down them. I didn't recoil but allowed him to stroke the tears away from my face. I opened my eyes again and realised that I was home in the front room of Cromford House. I was lying on the sofa.

I tried to move and sit up, but a pain shot through my shoulder. "Don't try to move," Robin said quickly as he put out a hand to stop me. "Your shoulder's been dislocated. The doctors put it back." he smiled shyly at me. "That's my fault I'm afraid. It popped when I grabbed you from the river."

"I don't understand," I said in a croaking, whispered voice. "You were there, why?"

Robin smiled and began to explain.

"I had promised Bill that I would go and get dog food from one of those pet superstores. That was why I couldn't see you tonight. I'd picked up some dog food and a few groceries from the supermarket for Bill on the way back. When I took them round, he told me that I had just missed you and that you had set off walking home. I was concerned. It was starting to get dark, and not exactly walking weather and I knew that your leg was troubling you, so I went to see if I could catch you up and give you a lift home. Why were you visiting Bill anyway?"

"I'll tell you later," I said.

Robin shrugged. "I saw Simon's Land Rover and thought that perhaps you had arranged for him to take you home when I saw you both crossing the meadow." He hesitated, looking a little ashamed. "I wondered what you were up too, so I followed you."

"When I saw Simon grab your hand, well. I knew that he wasn't being friendly."

Things started to shape in my mind. Robin had been the figure I had glimpsed. He had raced forward when I fell into the river, slipping and sliding to pull me from its grasp risking his own life to save mine. If he had hesitated for only a moment, then I would have been dragged under by the current and drowned.

"Simon's drowned," he whispered, "When I saw what he intended to do I tried to stop him, but I was too late, you had already fallen into the river. He tried to stop me from reaching you and we got into a fight. He lost his balance and toppled into the river, there was nothing I could do, and I needed to save you first." Robin let out a sigh and hung his head down. "I couldn't save you both."

I reached out and took his hand, when I became aware of someone quietly weeping. I struggled to crane my neck round without disturbing my shoulder to see where it was coming from.

I could see Raymond stood by the fireplace. He was clutching a glass with a large measure of whiskey, his face set in a grim expression. The fire was lit, and Duchess was laid out in front of it. I could see Lilian too, her face was pale, and tear stained, but it was Miranda that I could see was weeping.

She was sat on the small wooden stool that was by the fire, Lillian tightly held her in her arms comforting her like a forlorn child.

Lillian said something to Miranda, and she looked up with red swollen eyes and a blotchy face, sooty rivers of black mascara flowing down her cheeks.

All feelings of anger, disgust, and fear that I had harboured towards her disappeared in that instant and my heart went out to the pitiful creature that she had become.

"Simon and I were lovers," She began catching her breath. Lillian loosened her arms around Miranda and took hold of her hand, softly urging her to go on. With great effort, and trying to compose a little dignity she continued.

"We were going to marry, and reveal our relationship when Bobby passed away. We thought that it would be better to announce our plans after the funeral ... then there was all the trouble with the will ..." she faltered, as she clutched and unclutched a soggy tissue that she held. She cleared her throat. "Simon thought that it would be for the best if we kept our relationship secret for a while longer and then ... you turned up." She looked directly at me.

I saw no hatred in her face, nor any trace of animosity. She was a broken woman desperately trying to piece together the events and find reasons where no possible reason could be found.

She reached for another dry tissue to wipe away her tears, her poise and elegance briefly returning. "I could see that Simon was taken with you," she said, "you were so young and pretty, so fresh and an heiress!" She scoffed loudly. "And I was jealous!"

She paused and said in a much softer voice, "I knew in the details of the will if I was to have a child then they would inherit after Emily." Fresh tears welled up in Miranda's eyes, they sparkled and twinkled under the lights of the room. She swallowed hard and looked down at her hands. "I thought that if I told Simon I was pregnant, that he would have a son or a daughter … you see he was obsessed with the house, the estate; I thought if his child would eventually have everything, he would be satisfied with that and forget about Emily so I lied to him."

"Hell of a risk girl," Raymond muttered to her in a gruff voice.

Lillian shot him a glance that made Raymond fall silent. He took a gulp of his whiskey, his face glowing red with embarrassment.

Miranda ignored her father and continued, "Simon was delighted when I told him. I thought that now we would announce our engagement and arrange our wedding, but he was still reluctant.

When Emily returned to Cromford House in the spring Simon had changed. He had developed a hard edge that I had not noticed before. He was moody and distracted when we were together. I blamed Emily of course. And then I discovered that I was really expecting a child." Miranda turned to Lillian. "He really did love me, he really did." Her voice sounded anxious, convinced that her statement was true and looking for some form of reassurance that it was.

"I know," Lillian replied, forcing herself to smile and stroking Miranda's hair. "I know."

As I watched Lillian comfort Miranda, I cast my mind back over the last few months. Although the events stayed the same, I was now viewing them from a different perspective, rather like a familiar room that you unexpectedly see reflected in a mirror: everything the same, yet everything completely different.

Miranda's dislike of me had simply been because of her jealousy over Simon. I remembered the way she had stopped Simon from taking me to the train station and then some weeks later when he had come to pick me up, she gave some lame excuse over saving fuel. I also remembered the way she had insisted that she should accompany Simon and I on our walk to God's seat. And Simon's thinly disguised impatience with her.

Miranda had been radiant that day. Even the little quarrel that she and Simon had had over Robin hadn't lasted long. Her eyes had shone, her face was flushed pink and glowing, as the wind swept through her hair, there was a contentment about her, and I guessed now that she would have been pregnant. But how far – three maybe four months perhaps?

As though reading my mind Miranda broke into my thoughts and spoke.

"When we went up to God's seat, I had no idea ...no idea at all how desperate or fanatical Simon had become." She looked at me with wet, pleading eyes. "Please, Emily believe me. I never thought Simon intended to hurt you, to do what he intended to do, if those people hadn't have come when they did." Her voice trailed away into silence.

"What's this about God's seat?" Robin asked.

I shook my head. I didn't want to reply, not just yet.

I felt an odd sense of relief that I had been right about the attempt on my life that day, glad that I hadn't imagined it, but disturbed that it had been real, and Miranda's screams hadn't been for me; they had been for Simon when she realised the full intent and the of nature of his plans.

She had seen him push me – actually push me, and she knew that she was bound by that knowledge; unable to escape and trapped in a relationship with a man who was capable of murder to satisfy his own selfish greed.

"And the cellar?" I asked in a quiet, firm voice. "Who locked me in the cellar? Was that you?"

I could see Raymond and Lillian visibly stiffen; Robin wrapped a protective arm around me. I was driven by a thirst for the truth and a bold courage swept through me.

"No!" she gasped, horrified by the accusation. "No. Please believe me." She wailed. "I pleaded with him, begged him, to leave you alone. I told him we should get married and live in the house together. I would let him have my share of the estate and that you had no interest in the estate. I was going to give you the money for your business venture so you would be busy with that and well out of our way. That afternoon we were together. I had gone into the cellar for a bottle of champagne so that we could drink a toast to our new future as Simon had agreed to my idea. I had forgotten glasses, so Simon went to fetch some. You must have wandered into the cellar and then the idea came to him. I'd no idea what he had done, and it couldn't have been planned. I don't think that he intended to kill you. Just frighten you ..." her voice trailed off.

"Just frighten me?" I raised an eyebrow at her.

"He didn't tell me, and that night at the hospital when I realised what he had done, after you were found, I was terrified that he would try and do something stupid to harm you. So, I stayed with you all night, keeping a watch over you, praying that Simon would keep away.

"I thought that I had got through to him, to make him forget his evil plans. But I hadn't, had I?"

All this time I had believed that Miranda was the enemy, believing that she was manipulating Simon, yet the reverse was true. He had masterminded the whole thing and dragged an unwitting Miranda along in his wake.

His plan had been very simple: eliminate me, marry Miranda. The child would not have made much of a difference. Once he had married Miranda would she also have befallen a fatal accident, he was capable of one murder why not two, who knew what lengths his greed would go to.

"And the baby Raymond asked." His voice was gruff and unforgiving, but I could see the pain of his daughter's grief reflected in his face and the anguish that he felt at being unable to help her. The brusque way in which he spoke to her now was only an attempt to cover his feeling of grief, and helplessness.

Miranda sat very still staring into space, and said in a quiet voice barely above a whisper:

"I lost the baby."

Epilogue

The police were informed that Simon had fallen into the river. We all thought that it was for the best if we concealed the truth from them. No good would have come of us telling them the whole sorry tale. Simon was dead. He had paid the ultimate price for his greed. If we had disclosed the true facts of Simon's death it would have led to endless questioning, and we feared that Miranda may have been charged as an accessory to the attempts on my life. Robin too may have been charged with manslaughter as he and Simon had got into a fight on the river edge. That was something that I could not bear to contemplate, and Miranda had been through enough already. I could not allow Lillian and Raymond to go through such an ordeal with their daughter either. Simon had no next of kin. There was no need for anyone else to be involved or for anyone else to know the truth. Rightly or wrongly, we told the lie, and we would have to live with it, and we felt justified in doing so.

The story that we told the police was that we had gone to look at the swollen river and that Simon had been too bold and got too close. He lost his footing on the slippery ground and found himself overpowered by the flood waters. Robin and I had tried to help him, but I had slipped and plunged into the river during the rescue attempt. Robin had been able to save me, but it was too late for Simon.

It was some days later that Simon's battered body was found several miles downstream. Police divers had searched for his body once the river was safe for them to do so.

Raymond had the grim task of identifying the body. Lillian had taken Miranda away to Whitby on the east coast of Yorkshire hoping that the change of scene and the fresh sea air would help Miranda. I was glad that they were absent when the police came to tell us that Simon's body had been recovered.

As for myself, I had been advised to rest. I was battered and bruised from the debris that had hit me in the river, my shoulder was very sore where it had been dislocated, and my head ached. A tree branch had struck the side of my head causing me to black out when Robin had hauled me from the river: I was lucky that that alone hadn't killed me. I also had superficial cuts to my hands and arms, but my injuries would leave no lasting scars.

It was Miranda who would bear the real scars of my ordeal and they ran much deeper and would take far longer to heal than mine. She had really loved Simon. I couldn't help comparing her love and that of Edward Cromford for Evelyn. He too had risked everything for someone that he had loved. He had turned his back on his family, home, and way of life so that he could be with her. Edward knew that when he and Evelyn eloped there could be no turning back.

Miranda had taken similar risks to protect Simon from himself. The burden of her secret weighed her down and trapped her, but she never gave up on the man she loved however misguided his actions were. I would like to think that Simon had loved Miranda, and perhaps he had before greed had got in his way.

How strange this deep need for love. Like a secret, all powerful force within us. That drives us on with strength and courage. Sometimes, our need is so great that we follow a false love that blinds us and takes us on dangerous journeys into dark places and self-destruction. Perhaps that is our folly, this deep-seated desire to be loved that we let feelings of insecurity and fear consume our minds, when all we need to do is listen to our hearts. True love can only come from the heart. It never deceives us or tries to hurt us. It just guides us gently towards happiness if we choose to listen.

I sighed; would I know the difference? Do I listen to my heart?

There was a knock at the bedroom door.

"Come in," I said trying to sound cheerful and dispel the melancholy mood that had I had started to drift into.

Robin popped his head round the door, and I felt myself smile. He came in carrying a handful of flowers that looked as though they had been freshly picked from the garden. He was treading softly over the pale carpet in his socks (evidence of an encounter with Janice on the way up).

I struggled the best I could to sit up further in bed while Robin handed me the flowers: blue delphiniums, pale golden roses, and starry gypsophila.

I took the flowers from him, and they reminded me of a Victorian posy. I touched their velvet like petals and admired the intense blue of the delphiniums and the way that the gypsophila frothed over the golden roses. I smiled and put my face close to the flowers so I could inhale their fragrance. I felt gloriously alive.

"Be careful," Robin warned in a serious voice. I looked up. "I checked for earwigs, but you know what the little blighters are like, curling up all cosy and hiding in petals."

Robin was the most unromantic and conversely the most romantic man in the world.

He sat down on the edge of the bed and kissed me.

I closed my eyes and felt the love fill my heart. Yes, I thought, this was real love, and I knew it would never lead me astray down false paths. It was strong and true.

We pulled apart and I gazed up into his eyes. Once more I was drowning, but not in the cold clutches of a dark merciless river, but that of the blue green of a warm Caribbean Sea that were Robin's eyes. In that moment I realised that I had discovered my past, found a contentment in my present and I heard my heart whisper that I was looking directly into my future.

The end

HERZ FÜR AUTOREN A HEART FOR AUTHORS À L'ÉCOUTE DES AUTEURS MIA KAPΔIA ΓIA ΣYΓΓΡ
HARTA FÖR FÖRFATTARE UN CORAZÓN POR LOS AUTORES YAZARLARIMIZA GÖNÜL VERELIM SZ
ORE PER AUTORI ET HJERTE FOR FORFATTERE EEN HART VOOR SCHRIJVERS TEMOS OS AUTO
ZÕINKÉRT SERCE DLA AUTORÓW EIN HERZ FÜR AUTOREN A HEART FOR AUTHORS À L'ÉCOU
RAÇÃO ВСЕЙ ДУШОЙ К АВТОРАМ ETT HJÄRTA FÖR FÖRFATTARE Á LA ESCUCHA DE LOS AUTO
TEURS MIA KAPΔIA ΓIA ΣYΓΓΡΑΦΕΙΣ UN CUORE PER AUTORI ET HJERTE FOR FORFATTERE EEN
LARIMIZ ZÕINKÉRT SERCE DLA AUTORÓW EIN HERZ FÜ
SCHRIJ ÇÃO ВСЕЙ ДУШОЙ К АВТОРАМ ETT HJÄRTA FÖ

The author

Sharon Luty has always been enthusiastic about reading and creating stories.

She left school at 16 with a minimum of qualifications and no idea what she wanted to do with her life apart from a vague notion that she would like to write.

After many and various jobs Sharon now works in charity retail which she finds challenging, but also rewarding and fun.

She likes to be outdoors and loves walking; the Yorkshire countryside always offers beautiful settings for her stories.

Sharon enjoys taking part in steampunk events which combine her love of vintage fashion with her passion for classic cars.

Her newest interest is vintage car racing in a hot rod named "Little Yeller", which is providing inspiration for lots of future stories. Married for more than thirty years, she had three grown up children and lives in West Yorkshire. She enjoys gardening and cookery.